Museo
Kids

Miguel
Lost & Found
in the Palace

By Barbara Beasley Murphy

Illustrated by George Ancona

Museum of New Mexico Press
Santa Fe

Project editor: Mary Wachs
Design: David Skolkin
Manufactured in the United States of America
10 9 8 7 6 5 4 3 2 1

Library of Congress Cataloging-in-Publication Data Available

Museum of New Mexico Press
Post Office Box 2087
Santa Fe, New Mexico 87504

Dedication

To my son, Andrea Alberto Mammoli,
with admiration and love.

In memory of a blessed friend,
Joanne San Antonio Hoppe (1932–2001)

Acknowledgments

For inspiration and support for *Miguel Lost & Found in the Palace:* Kind Readers Joanne San Antonio Hoppe, Emily Harburg, Jennifer Murphy Mammoli, Bill Murphy, Sylvia Beasley Snyder, Cookie Jordan, Sue Sturtevant, Anna Gallegos, Mary Wachs, Lou Ann Shurbet, Libby Sternberg, Diane de Santis, Pamela Kelly, and Tom Chavez. Fine Writers: Susan Hazen-Hammond, Yolanda Nava, Ana Castillo, the members of No Poets, and Denise Chavez; Anne Constable, Marc Simmons, and others at the *New Mexican.*

Part One

BOYS ON THE
BORDER BETWEEN

1

Joey. Miguel.

On the giant bridge between Juárez, Mexico, and El Paso, Texas, spotlights turned night into day. They shone on Sergeant Richard Cortés wearing a snappy INS Border Patrol uniform and picking fajita meat out of his teeth. He popped spit over the rail into the waters of the Rio Grande below. The river, whispering *swisha swisha swisha*, separated Mexico from the U.S.A.

Over the cars creeping across the bridge, the sergeant heard his partner, the lieutenant, calling. "Hurry up, man!"

"One minute, sir!"

Brushing his black, nipped mustache, Sergeant Cortés checked the green jacket buttoned across his full belly. Nothing had dripped on it. Easy to see he looked as terrific as ever.

His duty was to stop illegal traffic into the U.S. It gave him the chance to snoop in every car stopped for inspection. He searched for hidden drugs, fruits, vegetables, pets and birds, *and* for people sneaking across the border without documentation. He stopped both illegal and legal travelers. Women, especially, he would tell you, moaned and cried if they were caught without legal papers and sent home again. Little kids boohooed, reminding him of his five year old, Joey Jeter Cortés.

His kid did *not* boohoo. That kid was a great little man. He could sock a baseball into outer space. Sergeant Cortés was teaching him. His dream for Joey Jeter was that someday he'd star in the Majors. Get money and fame big time. Yes!

Sergeant Cortés dreamed of being a baseball star himself. But as hot an athlete as he was, he didn't get good at the game. He blamed his father. Señor Cortés hadn't taught *him* to bat at the formative age of five. Instead the old man had taken little Richard to *Luna Cocina,* or Moon Kitchen, where he cooked day and night. He made his son learn that.

But cooking wasn't for Richard. No!

He wasn't going to work in small, smelly kitchens. He wasn't a Mexican anymore either. He never admitted to anyone, not even his wife, that his family had once been illegal aliens. No! He was Texan now, a naturalized citizen. Yes! He graduated from the INS Academy, the youngest to be appointed. Yes, yes, yes!

Sergeant Richard Cortés held the record for uncovering illegal people. He had turned back hundreds of them.

"Proud of you, Sergeant Sweetie!" his wife, Mrs. Charlotte Cortés, would say, her upturned red nose and long white chin held high.

His freckle-faced boy got the message, too. Just yesterday a little *mojado,* a "wetback," yelled at rusty-haired Joey Jeter. Joey popped him, leaving the kid bawling on the day-care center floor.

Thinking of it, Sergeant Richard Cortés (and don't you call him Ricky either!) chuckled.

If he got his way, this bridge would become **impervious**. No illegal fool sneaking out of Mexico to steal an American job would get across.

"Hey! I need me a cup a coffee," the lieutenant yelled across the line of stopped cars again. "Break's over, Ricky!"

Sergeant Richard Cortés's face flushed chile-pepper red. "Right away, sir!" he shouted, saluting. He arced a last spit into the river. "Get 'em, tough guy!" he said to himself. Snapping his fingers, stepping smartly, he zipped back to the business of the night.

Thirty-five miles east of the bridge over the Rio Grande, a man in a heavy sweatshirt, jeans, and worn-out sneakers waded into the water. Crístobal Rivera was carrying his son on his shoulders, tightening a thin blanket around him.

Miguel Rivera was five years old just like Joey Jeter Cortés on the other side of the border. His father steadied Miguel with a hand on his bare knee; the other held his wife's hand. Rosa Rivera was shaking with fear. Little Miguel pressed his lips between his teeth. The only sound as they moved through the water was *swisha swisha swisha*.

Rising, the water reached Miguel's shoes, soaking his sneakers and socks, wetting his feet. He could feel Papa shivering. Suddenly there was a big splash. His mama had tripped and fallen into the river. But suddenly again, her head rose out of the water. She stood up.

She didn't say a thing, Miguel thought. His mother was a talker, always shouting what she thought. But not tonight! This was different. Miguel pinched his own busy lips tighter.

They stopped to let her catch her breath. The *swisha swisha swisha* stopped, too. Gasps were all Miguel heard. The desert air smelled of chemicals and engine exhaust and the river.

A coyote howled. Rosa Rivera gasped. Under Miguel's legs, his father's shoulders stiffened. His mother's teeth were chattering loud enough for Miguel to hear. He pictured the wild coyote running up and down the riverbank, its ears back, neck fur bristling.

There was no moon and just a spray of six tiny stars behind them. Ahead lay a thick darkness. A gray line in the eastern sky was like a scribble Miguel had made on *DIARIO X*, the secret newspaper.

Slowly the Riveras moved forward.

"The only way we can cross the Rio Grande and keep the border patrol from catching us and slamming us into jail is to be soft
as light on water. Silent as the fishes swimming in it," Miguel's
father had said before they started out at three o'clock this Monday afternoon. He said the words in Spanish, then in the English
he had learned working at Fort Bliss in El Paso before he married
Rosa. She and Miguel promised they understood the need for
absolutely no talking.

They had taken a long bus ride from Ciudad Juárez, Mexico,
the city connected to the guarded bridge. In their wood pallet and
cardboard house without water or electricity, they had planned
their illegal move to the United States.

They were leaving Mexico to begin a new life. Hungry and
poor, Miguel's parents could not find work in their country. They
had no education that would allow them to enter the United
States legally. They believed that there were jobs they could do
well in the United States, so they'd earn enough to live on and feel
safe again.

Crossing the Rio Grande now, they heard the coyote's yelp again.
Funny there's only one, Miguel thought. Coyotes ran in packs,
yelping and scrapping over prey. Was the coyote alone on the
riverbank that they were coming to but could not see? If it were,
Miguel thought it must be starving.

Coyotes had packed the rising hills near his *tia's* house in
Zacatecas. They preyed on chickens, rabbits, and even dogs.
Miguel had watched a man shoot a coyote dead once. He carried
it home and cut off its tail. In the market at Miguel's aunt's fruit
stand, it sold for sixty pesos.

And then Tía Yolanda Ana had died of pneumonia. The house
that Miguel's family had lived in with her had been taken by the
owners. There was no place for *la familia Rivera* to live anymore.

Miguel's feet were cold. In the sky the line had grown as wide
as his finger. Papa's breathing was harder, his shoulders and neck
as stiff as a bull's. They waded out and the water ran down their
legs in rivulets.

"*Gracias a Dios!* Thanks to God," his father whispered, walking straight ahead as if he could see the way in front of them. They were moving fast. And then running. Miguel, bouncing on his father's shoulders, held tight.

They rushed into darkness, his mother's and father's shoes thudding on the ground. With an ankle twisted in her fall in the river, Rosa tripped and fell again. She was up and running immediately.

Hard, rapid breathing was the only sound. Miguel, clinging to Papa's neck, jumped at the whine of an unknown animal to the right. His father turned and ran in that direction. Mama, behind them, was panting in the struggle to keep up. Miguel's eyes strained against the dark. *Is she following? Did something get her?*

And then they heard a low whistle. Two deep notes followed by three high ones. His father, recognizing it, took a deep, deep breath. His mother, catching up, let out a moan of relief.

Miguel bit his lip when he heard his mother's "Aaahhh!"

The whistle signaled that their *Amiga*, Friend for the Crossing, was there. They recognized the notes of the whistle. It belonged to the Zacatecas neighborhood. The *Amiga* had moved away from Zacatecas. All the *compadres and comadres* there used the same whistle to call one another. If you heard it, you'd know it was your friend or relative calling. Sometimes it signaled danger. Tonight it signaled rescue.

Crístobal and Rosa Rivera stopped moving. The gray line in the sky widened, becoming as thick as Miguel's arm.

He heard footfalls. And then he was taken from his father into the arms of a woman smelling of perfume and sweat and something sugary. She kissed his cheek, giving him a candy to suck.

"*Para ti, niño.* For you, brave boy," she whispered in his ear, the warm breath tickling his skin. It was hard for Miguel to open his tight-shut lips to take the cherry candy inside his dry mouth.

The woman and her daughter immediately pulled the Riveras over to a van. Its doors were open but the interior lights weren't lit. In silence they climbed inside, closing the doors with an almost silent click.

The engine growled and turned over. It sounded weak and worn out. Miguel was being undressed in the backseat next to the big woman. She was pulling off his wet river shoes and throwing them out the window with all of his other wet clothes. A sweater was buttoned around him, blankets wrapped tightly over that, warming him.

His mother and father threw their shoes away, too, and hid in the back under piles of burlap chile bags. The scent of spicy, roasted chiles filled their noses. He remembered he was hungry. Thirsty. His mother's teeth were still chattering. *Maybe Mama's crying.*

The younger Amiga, Friend for the Crossing, drove the van. She used no headlights to see but bent forward, her face to the windshield. They raced away from the river as the darkness faded. After fifteen minutes of bumping over hard ground and spinning out of control two or three times, the van rolled onto a paved street.

Everybody sighed, the smoothness felt so nice.

"We're here?" Miguel said in Spanish.

"Almost. A little more. Then you go into a warm bed. It's waiting just for you," the driver said. They didn't know her name, only that she was from Zacatecas. They were not told the other Amiga's name either.

The car took a sharp right into a driveway and drove straight into an open garage attached to the house. Before the engine was turned off, a man inside slammed the garage door. Miguel saw his brown, serious face. His iron gray hair was lit by a triangle of light coming from an inside room.

Wasting no time, everybody climbed out of the car and into the room. It had a window that let in gray light. They were given water to drink. Miguel's father put on ragged jeans and a dusty, soiled sweatshirt. Rosa put on khaki pants and a blue work shirt. The young Amiga silently dressed Miguel in red lacy pajamas.

"These are girl's pants," he whispered to her.

"Ssshh! A disguise for you. You have to look like my niece."

The large Amiga was chopping off Rosa's long black hair with scissors. Tears that she squeezed back stood in her eyes. Miguel, sad for her, wanted to put his arms around her. The front of her clothes was stuffed to make her look like a fat man instead of a woman. A straw hat was pushed over her head. Just for today each person in Miguel's family was taking the place of someone who lived in the community legally. That is why his mother was disguised as a man. The Amigas for the Crossing had made the plan in advance, paying these people to help the Riveras with the money Miguel's father had sent.

Crístobal Rivera's head was shaved bald and a stocking cap pulled over it. "My shirt says 'Dallas Power and Light,' Miguel," he whispered.

All three Riveras were given brand new sneakers. They were the right sizes.

"*Adios, Mami!*" Miguel said, when his mother kissed him.

"*Mi corazón, mi 'jito!*" Rosa Rivera said. "Back soon."

He worried she was kissing him too much. They could get caught.

"Come on! Come on!" the man who locked the door growled.

Rosa left with the large Amiga who smelled only of sweat now, not perfume. She said, "I'm taking Rosa to a meat-packing factory. She'll work in my brother's place. A grounds-keeper."

"She is tired. She is going to have a baby this summer," Crístobal pleaded. "Please tell them to watch out for her."

"Don't worry, *hombre*. She can sleep in the bus on the way. It's forty miles from here."

Then they were gone.

Miguel's father kissed him, squeezing him so tight that Miguel coughed. "Be strong, *mi 'jito*. I'll come back to you. Tonight."

Miguel nodded. He did not cry.

The gray-haired man shoved open a window. It was first light. Miguel's father threw a leg over the sill, slid down and ran across the backyard. He jumped a wall and climbed onto a sanitation truck stopped there, grinding its screeching gears. It took off with Crístobal Rivera and the other men collecting garbage. They disappeared into the pink dawn.

The window was closed and the light turned off. The escape car driver lifted Miguel into her arms. Through a door in the dark garage, she carried him into the house. She laid him in a child's bed there.

"Today just call me Mama, and don't say nothing else. You are supposed to be sick. My husband has taken our little niece to his friend's nursery school. We are pretending you are our María. As soon as we're sure nothing is going wrong with the plan, I can give you food, some breakfast, Miguel . . . I mean, María."

Miguel whispered to the woman in Spanish, "How does she smile?"

"What?"

"María? Does she smile big or little?"

"Ahh! Not too much," the woman said sadly. "Her real mama's in prison. She was caught on the border."

Miguel pressed his lips closed again and nodded. His mother and father had told him that all of these things would happen to him. Staying with an unknown family. Pretending to be somebody else. It felt strange. The house smelled a little pewy, too, at least not like the homes he knew. He was not supposed to be scared. He had to be good in every way. So he tried to like it. The people were nice.

No say nothing, he said to himself in the English he was trying to understand a little bit. Like María, whose pajamas he was wearing, he stopped smiling much.

2

El Paso del Norte/

The Pass to the North

Three years after arriving in the little farm town in Texas, the dreams of Miguel's family were coming true. His father had been hired for work after his first scary day in the garbage-collecting job. His mother found an old industrial sewing machine in a junk shop. They bought it for $72.39. Crístobal Rivera had been able to save that much in a few months.

In the secret illegal-immigrant house, he and Rosa started a small business sewing pot holders and pillowcases. Then they moved to the old border town of El Paso. It had good schools. They found an apartment with both a furnace and plumbing. Piped water was still a miracle. Every day, Miguel, eight, climbed into the cold hard shiny white bathtub.

If nobody says nothing, I'll fill it all the way to the top.

But water running alerted his mother. She worked in the hall next to the bathroom, where the sewing machine was set up. So she heard everything. "Don't waste nothing!" she screamed outside the door. "Water no is free! We will run out of it, *'jito!*"

"I can't get away with nothing!" Miguel screamed back, turning off the tap. "You got to be clean in third grade."

"Already you clean!" she shouted louder. "And late for the school."

"No, Mama! I am the first one every day," Miguel yelled. He

opened the door and showed himself fully dressed, socks, shoes, and all. His brown hair was as slick as tar, his smile as big as the sun.

"You too fast for me, *mi 'jito!*" Rosa said, laughing and trying to hug him as he shot past and ran out the door.

One day Rosa Rivera dreamed a big dream. At breakfast on a hot September Saturday, she was telling all about it.

"*Ayy!* I dream I am in *la ciudad de Santa Fe*. Santa Fe is the capital of New Mexico, *niños*. I seen real pictures. Beautiful! Up in mountain clouds. In winter, the white snow it comes down . . ." Rosa sighed like she was hungry. "I dream I am wearing the violet ski suit. I have the red . . . gloves . . . um . . . mittens. The furred hat. Is gorgeous!"

Miguel grinned. "YOU in a ski suit, Mom?" Miguel laughed.

"Miguel. I dream I was sliding! You know, sliding on skis. Very . . ." She waved her hand to show how slippery the skis were. "Wissshhh! Down *la montaña*."

Miguel squinched his eyes, trying to see his mother this way.

"I remember the skiing from when I was a *niña*, just a girl."

Miguel laughed. "No, you don't! You never skied, Mom."

"Yes, I **do.** It was a film in México! I no forget that film. Pedro Enfante was the star. Is in my heart. Is my dream!"

"I can learn skiing, too, Mom!" Miguel said.

His father said, "Not **me!** I don't like cold. I'll go to Santa Fe and be a *santero*." He had carved wooden figures in Mexico and sold some. In El Paso, however, he worked as a night watchman in an automobile parts factory. It did not have anything to do with carving wood.

"I'll learn to be a *santero*, too," Miguel said.

Everybody in the family laughed. Miguel always wanted to do what everybody else wanted to do. He loved what made other people happy.

But everybody knew he was no good with his hands. His writing was terrible. He got D's in art. He couldn't catch a ball. He knocked things over, spilled food on the table or the floor, tripped

on his own boots and fell down. He'd learned the English word
clumsy the hard way, by bumping into the wrong people. He'd
been bumped back hard.

Mama explained his clumsiness by saying, "Miguel grew too
fast in this new country. Too much good food."

"What's a *santero?*" one of his twin sisters asked her father.

"A wood carver who makes holy figures or pictures," Crístobal
said.

The other twin said, "We'll be *santeras.*"

Oprah and Carla were three and were born in the United States
six months after Miguel's family crossed the Rio Grande. They
were named for women his mother liked best on television, Oprah
Winfrey and Carla Aragón. Rosa was so grateful for them. The
TV helped her learn English and she was so determined to do it
that everyone had to speak English almost all the time in the
house.

"We live here in Texas. We speak English so that I can be a big
success in work," she said. "I cannot make no more mistakes,
Miguel. You hear me?" Rosa said proudly, a smile on her face. "I
can speak like the TV. Some people say TV is a bad thing. You
believe it? They don't have no need for TV like me and you. No! I
no say TV is bad. Is a gift from heaven. I love it. It make my homesick go away."

Miguel would start to giggle because Mama's eyes would shine
and her face looked beautiful. He noticed she would not use her
Spanish except for necessities—like telling somebody off who had
cheated her or to describe her love for something or somebody.

She was studying to become a naturalized citizen, too.

The other person who shared the three-room apartment in El
Paso was María Contenta. She was the child whose red lacy pajamas Miguel had worn after the secret crossing of the river. The
disguise would have protected him from discovery as an outsider
if the border patrol had searched for illegals on their first day in
the United States. María, too, was eight, like Miguel.

Her mother had died in prison a month after Miguel and his

family moved into the house where María lived. No one knew her father. Out of thankfulness for finding a life in the United States, Rosa and Crístobal had taken the orphan child as one of their own and loved her.

Miguel watched out for her. She suffered sadness, or depression, and sometimes talked to nobody. Except him.

It was the first day of school after the Columbus Day holiday, *el día de la raza*. The children were picking up their lunches in brown bags and their schoolbooks. The Tortugas School was three short blocks away from home. Miguel's sisters, who were in nursery school, always ran all the way there. Miguel usually slowed down the last block so the twins could win. It made them happy the whole day.

María Contenta stayed home with Rosa and Crístobal. He was trying to help the girl learn to sew little pot holders out of pretty fabrics. On some days she could do three of them. On other days, feeling scared and alone, she stared at the wall.

3

An Enemy Behind

The third grade class in Tortugas School had a man for a teacher. He was probably the tallest teacher in third grade history. He had to duck when he entered the classroom because he was six inches taller than the door frame. The kids, except for two tall boys, only came up to Mr. Springley's belt.

He had played basketball in college and was a little bit famous in El Paso. But he said, "Basketball's nothin' as fun as teachin' little kids in school. My passion's history," he told his pupils. "I'm going to stuff you young folks full of history before I get old."

Miguel cringed. He hated history.

The teacher told them he was twenty-three. Of course someone that old liked history. He was ancient.

"I expect to have a Texas governor come out of my class one day. I expect to have a poet laureate, too, even though you don't know what that is yet. And . . . and . . ." he said, his red eyebrows bristling over his glasses. They made him look like an owl. But a nice owl.

". . . And an American president," he said. "It's all right with me if she's a girl. But that doesn't let you boys off the hook. Because I'm here to prepare leaders, there's a lot you have to know. Use your memory. We're gonna pack it full. To practice memorizin', you can learn the names of all the players in the World Series this month. By the end of the year, you'll have to know the names of all the Texas governors and the United States presidents. If you were born in Mexico, you will need to know also . . . I said ALSO, *NOT*

INSTEAD, to also know the names of your Mexican presidents."

"I know 'em! I know 'em, I already know 'em," Miguel said, shooting his arm up in the air. "I learned 'em last night, Mr. Springley."

Mr. Springley spread out his huge hands and waved them like directional flags at a plane. "Sshh, Miguel! I didn't say *right away*. This week we're watching the playoffs at night. We don't have time for the presidents yet. Save your knowledge, my smart and fine friend."

Miguel beamed. He felt good until a fist socked him on the back, attacking him. He wheeled around in his seat.

A red-haired boy with brown eyes, fat freckles, a tiny nose, and a mouth twisted in a mean scowl kept hitting him.

Miguel put his arms up to stop the attack. "Don't hit me, Joey Jeter. I didn't do nothing to you."

"Snot nose!" Joey Jeter Cortés hissed, leaning over and punching Miguel's shoulder another two times. "You act so smart. You show off! You're dumb. You were supposed to watch the Arizona Diamondbacks and the Yankees last night. I saw it. So did Webb and Adam and everybody else on my team."

Webb and Adam were sitting in their rows on either side of Joey. He was the biggest boy in class. He had a sweaty smell Miguel tried not to notice.

Miguel felt his face get as hot as a habanero chile pepper. "What team is it?"

"My champion team. I'm going to tell the teacher you didn't watch TV and didn't do the assignment." He pinched Miguel's wrist, making tears pop into his eyes.

Miguel spun around, hoping Joey Jeter could not see how embarrassed he was. The true facts were very sad, but they were very true.

Our TV's busted. Dad and Mom can't buy a new one. We need a new sewing machine. I can't see no world serious games like the other kids.

4

A Sickening Substitution

Miguel found a big bruise staring him in the face when he jumped out of the bathtub Wednesday morning. He had twisted around to look at his back in the mirror. He found one on his chin, too. The kid knocking him around in the classroom also used him for punching at recess.

Miguel made a plan while sitting on the side of the tub and drying off.

I'm not going to say nothing to that kid. I'll stay a million miles away from him. In school I will seek a change in my desk seat. If he socks me one more time, I'm not going to say nothing to him. I will go to Mr. Springley. I will be the tattletale. He will get a month of detention! He will fail, be left back . . .all the way back. In kindergarten!

Miguel laughed so hard he rolled back into the tub and bumped his head. Then he shoved himself out again and brushed his teeth vigorously. He was using baking soda and salt. They were saving money on toothpaste this month. He looked glumly in the foggy mirror. But a face suddenly appeared in it and smiled at him. He smiled back.

It said, *You can't say nothing to the teacher, Miguel Rivera. It will make big trouble. Joey Jeter's friends: that brown-haired show-off Adam and that skinny grouch, Webb. They will try to beat you up, too.*

"I don't want nothing, Face-in-the-Mirror, except to be a friend," Miguel answered.

The steam face was fading quickly. His own serious brown eyes with their black eyelashes appeared. And then his strong cheek-bones. They revealed he had the blood of Maya kings mixing proudly with the blood of Spanish *conquistadores* in his veins. He raised his arms and his biceps showed. *I have a straight nose, thick black hair, and dark skin. People, not just my mother, say I am as handsome as a Mexican cowboy.*

"I don't have new clothes, Face-in-the-Mirror. See? I don't look good to kids. So they hit me. I need a baseball team cap. To be cool. Like the other kids. Not so poor. Joey Jeter has a baseball cap for every team in the USA." He shook his head sadly.

He stared into the mirror. Why it don't say nothing more?

Running to school with Carla and Oprah, Miguel didn't slow down that morning.

"Sorry, little sisters! Today I can't lose the race. Don't be mad, okay? There's your teacher, waving hands at you. Go to her."

"Miguel! Miguel!" they screamed in one loud voice. "Wait up! wait up!"

He zoomed ahead. In the playground he searched for his tormentor. Not a sign of Joey Jeter Cortés.

He is sick? No? Not in school? Not in the playground. Yippee!

Without waiting for the bell to ring, Miguel ran inside the one-story brick building. It smelled like chalk and paint and fajita meat and pinto beans and red and green chile cooking in the lunchroom. Two people on ladders were in the hallway rolling white paint on the dingy ceiling. They were arguing about the New York Yankees.

Miguel was thinking. I can say to the teacher, *Mr. Springley, this is private. Sorry, but I can't see the baseball games, Mr. Springley. I know you assigned for the students, yes. I know, but the TV in my house is busted.*

He likes kids. He likes me, too. He will listen. I will tell him I feel like an estupido. He will say, don't feel bad about anything, Miguel. You are very, very good in reading. You are not so good in the art or history, but you can study when you want to. He told me that. It was nice of him.

He means it.

But when Miguel walked into the classroom, he found a woman sitting in the teacher's chair, sitting at Mr. Springley's very own desk. Miguel stopped in the door. "Where is Mr. Springley?"

The woman looked up in surprise. Her cheeks got fiery red. She did not look pleased. She did not answer him.

Didn't she hear me? Miguel thought. *My voice is not strong? Her ears are not listeners?* He stood there, heart racing.

The woman kept sitting.

"Is the teacher sick? He didn't have no accident, did he? He is not my teacher no more?" he finally said in a nervous rush, looking from the woman and then into the unbearable smirk of Joey Jeter Cortés.

That big kid, wearing a Yankee team baseball hat over his stringy red hair, was washing the chalkboard with a gray, drippy rag. And making a mess. Miguel suddenly noticed that the woman at the desk had a big smirk on her face, too. It was exactly like the one on the kid. Miguel's eyes opened wide. An awful thought came into his head.

They are here to say private stuff to the teacher? To say lies about me? Maybe so.

The woman was wearing a big brown felt hat. She wheeled around in her chair and yelled at Miguel, "Get your grammar straight, third grader!" The red blotches on her face got redder.

"Excuse me, Mrs. . . . ?" he said.

"NOT he didn't have NO accident. But, he didn't have AN accident. And not teacher NO MORE. It's ANYMORE," the woman said. She had the longest chin Miguel had ever seen. What was worse, it did not match her little nose.

Miguel was trembling. He could not remember saying NO MORE. He was sure he had said ANYMORE. He could not remember the first thing she just told him. He did not know why his words made her mad.

"Who is this boy?" she said to Joey Jeter Cortés, swabbing the marker trays.

"Nobody. He just sits in front of me," Joey Jeter said to the woman sitting at Mr. Springley's desk like she belonged there. He was swabbing the board with too much water. Big chalky puddles formed on the red Mexican tile floor.

The woman pointed to the door. "The bell hasn't rung, third grader. Get back outside."

"But what about him? Why's Joey Jeter here?" Miguel burst out, an awful feeling dawning on him. Unfortunately the feeling did not hit him soon enough—the feeling that he should keep his mouth shut. That he should do just what the lady in the desk chair had ordered.

"He gets to be here because **He** is my son, Joey Jeter Cortés. I asked him to show me the way to the classroom where I'm substituting today."

Miguel not only wished he'd run back to the playground like the scary substitute had ordered, he wished he had gone further than that. He wished he had flown straight home.

The bell rang as words came stuttering out of Miguel's mouth. "Well, well, well nothing's not wrong with Mr. Springley, is it?"

"Is *there*! Not *is it*! There's nothing wrong with Mr. Springley, is THERE? Remember that and go to your seat!" Mrs. Charlotte Cortés commanded. "Enough questions."

Miguel dropped his head low and ran to his seat. He was scared. How could he remember THERE? He did not understand what he had said that was bad and so wrong. His heart sank. He wished he could help Mr. Springley get better, so he'd come back to Tortugas School and save him from that scary substitute with the popping-at-him eyes.

5

Somebody's Out!

Miguel Rivera found himself at bat for the first time in his life. He was playing in a one-inning baseball game at Tortugas School. There were two outs on his side already. The other team had one run, made by Joey Jeter Cortés in the first two seconds of the game. He had been first up to bat.

Mrs. Charlotte Cortés had decided to teach the game of baseball to her pupils. She had now taken off the big brown hat and put on a Dodgers cap. It made her look like a bird Miguel had seen long ago in Mexico. His little friends in Zacatecas had called it the peepee bird. Who knew why? He did know he was glad his mother did not have a brown hat, or a baseball cap. That she just wore her beautiful long hair.

"Mr. Springley never taught you sports, pupils," Mrs. Cortés the Substitute had announced that morning as though it was a crime. It was the Friday of the second week that Mr. Springley had disappeared from the third grade class at Tortugas.

Now more than likely, Miguel thought, Mr. Springley is dead. *Nobody's saying nothing to us kids. We're not really afraid of death but big people think so. We can know about it. It's okay. It's life and death for everybody. I just want Mr. Springley to be okay. To come back to his students. I need to tell him the presidentes of Mexico. I never got to say it once even.*

Miguel wanted also to explain to Mrs. Cortés that Mr. Springley had, too, taught them sports. He taught jogging, and stretching, and kicking out and jumping up and down, and push-ups. Mr. Springley felt there was never enough time to play games like baseball and basketball at recess.

Miguel wanted to explain, but his mouth had stopped opening in class. He could not say verbs or anything right. And it made Mrs. Cortés-the-Scary-Substitute hopping mad when she asked him a question and he couldn't answer. He was getting a bunch of zeroes. *I can't say nothing.* And when he tried to tell his mother that something was wrong with his talking, and that his speech was bad, it made her furious at Mrs. Cortés-the-Scary-Substitute. Mom threatened to come to school and talk to her.

Rosa Rivera's tongue was hot. She would try to tell Mrs. Cortés off. But it wouldn't be in English, Miguel knew. No! Much worse! It would be in Spanish. The many syllabled words would cut Mrs. Cortés like a knife, wounding her, as they sometimes did him. And Mama, still an illegal alien, would get arrested and put in jail and who knows what else. So Miguel stopped complaining at home.

"You talk perfect just like me," his mother said every day after she had first heard of his problem. " Nothing is not wrong with your speech because I teached you every little thing I was teached from the TV by Carla Aragón and Oprah Winfreed."

"Taught," said Miguel.

Rosa glared at him, black eyes like coals, and told him, "Just shut up!" She was shaking.

So now on this Friday afternoon recess, for the first time in his life, Miguel was up at bat in a baseball game. Joey Jeter, who was still punching him around, was playing shortstop.

Miguel knew he was clumsy and didn't know anything for sure about baseball, but he decided to try his best anyway. Joey, Adam, and Webb wouldn't let him win anyway. He took a deep breath. The first ball was pitched to him by a new kid in third grade, Tim Blume.

Tim didn't open his mouth in class either. Miguel had never even heard his voice. He had come from Africa two weeks after school had opened. He was not a black African. He was a white

African and looked just like most white people from Texas did.

But Tim looked Miguel straight in the eye today. Miguel guessed that Tim wanted him to make the ball fly. Tim fired the ball hard. It came straight as an arrow.

Miguel swung the bat just as hard. The bat connected with a crack. The ball sailed into the air, bouncing inches from Joey Jeter Cortés, the shortstop. He knelt down to scoop it into his glove. The kids were screaming. The ball rolled and flipped off a rock on its way into the air again.

Joey Jeter was trying to get his fingers around the ball, when it hit the rock, popped up, and smacked him in the face.

By then Miguel had rounded first base and was heading for second.

Adam and Webb and the other kids on Joey Jeter's team were yelling, "Joey! Get the ball! You shoulda got 'im out!"

They laughed when Joey Jeter stood up, red-faced, tears squirting out of his eyes.

And then they yelled, "Joey, throw the ball. Come on! Awww!" But by then Miguel was on third base, thinking of home plate.

Joey Jeter dropped the ball, picked it up, and heaved it at the pitcher. Instead of watching the shortstop on *his* team throw the ball to him, Timothy Blume, the pitcher, was watching Miguel sail around the bases. Tim had a smile on his face, too.

The face of Mrs. Charlotte Cortés the Substitute was a firecracker ready to explode.

"Time out! Game over!" she cried when Miguel was just a couple yards from home plate. "Everybody back in the classroom."

"But Miguel's about to make a run!" Timothy Blume yelled. "You can't stop the game before he gets home."

Miguel blinked. The African kid spoke good English.

"Whose side are you on!" Joey Jeter and the rest of the guys yelled at him.

At that moment Miguel stepped on home plate.

"Recess is over, third grader," Mrs. Cortés the Substitute yelled at Tim. "And *you'll* stay after school for insubordination," she said.

"Recess is over."

The kids in Mr. Springley's class moaned and looked at each other as though they were on one team and Mrs. Charlotte Cortés the Substitute was on the other. Joey Jeter Cortés slunk into the school behind his mother.

When Miguel got to his seat, he was still panting from excitement. *Nothing ever felt as good as socking that ball into the sky.* He relived every second of running around the field, his feet stepping lightly on the base bags. Chalk squeaked on the board. Mrs. Charlotte Cortés the Substitute was writing a long list there.

Inoculation, she wrote. **Epidemic. Diphtheria. Plague. Hemorrhage. Coronary Infarction.**

Adam and Webb and some other kids giggled at that, looking from one to the other across Joey Jeter's desk.

"Copy every single word into your blue notebooks. Get the definitions from your dictionaries at home tonight. Write each one in a sentence. There is going to be a spelling bee on these words after a written test tomorrow," Mrs. Cortés said.

Miguel stared at the words. To him they looked like a hospital list. He glanced over at Tim Blume in the second row, who rolled his eyes up to heaven.

Miguel giggled and felt a bang and two clumps on his head. Joey Jeter was clobbering him with his big textbook.

"Hey! That hurt!" Miguel said, turning around in time to get a pencil point poked in his nose.

"Miguel Rivera!" Mrs. Cortés the Substitute shouted. "You are not to look on somebody else's paper. Turn around! Do your own work or you'll stay after school with Timothy Blume."

He couldn't stay after school because he had to walk his sisters home every day. He tried to speak, but his mouth would not open.

"Be up at my desk when the bell rings."

Which it did immediately. Everybody slammed their notebooks shut and roared out of the room. Miguel had put only three of the words down on his paper, so he sat there trying to catch up.

Psychosis, he wrote.

Immunosuppressant.

Enema

He was biting his lip, hurrying to finish. "e m a . . ." he whispered to be sure he had the letters right. "Ouch!" he suddenly yelled.

On his way down the aisle, Joey Jeter stomped on Miguel's foot, saying, "Get you later, freak. You're not gonna get away with your black magic, making that ball jump into my face. I got a bruise. I'm going to have to go to the doctor. If my mother makes me go, I'm going to punch out your eyes and spit in the sockets."

Miguel felt an electric current jump up and down his body. He wanted to grab Joey Jeter and knock him down. But it was too late. Joey Jeter was up front letting Mrs. Charlotte Cortés the Substitute kiss him good-bye.

"Go straight home, Sweetie. I have to stay here with these bad boys," she said, turning off her smile. She looked at Miguel, her face now long and sour as a pickle.

Miguel was determined to leave. He knew that Oprah and Carla waited at the corner of the school yard. "Please, Mrs.," he was able to whisper. "My little sisters are three years old. They need . . . um . . . my mother says to . . . um . . ."

"Finish your sentence!" she screamed.

Miguel's face got as hot as a furnace. "I gotta go!" he said and ran out the door before she could stop him.

Down in the playground he grabbed Oprah's and Carla's hands and started running home as fast as they could go.

At the second corner they waited until two fire engines with sirens going roared past them. They had to catch their breath anyway. Miguel was telling them why he was a little late meeting them. They stopped holding hands and walked slowly across the street with its neat little houses on either side. It was pretty hot and they looked forward to the one big cottonwood tree in the middle of the block, shading the sidewalk.

When they reached the tree, Joey Jeter Cortés and Adam and Webb and three boys from fourth grade jumped out from behind an adobe wall. They scared his sisters to death.

"Booooo!" they yelled, making the two little girls burst into tears.

"Chicanos! Mojados. Wetbacks!" the bigger boys yelled, making faces. "Go home. Back to Mexico! We don't want you here. You stink.

You can't speak English," they said.

"We can so," Oprah shouted, running up and pounding the biggest one with her little fists.

As suddenly as they'd appeared, the boys ran off.

Miguel ran after Joey Jeter, reaching his hand out and grabbing the back of his baseball jacket with all the team emblems on it. The material ripped and stuck to Miguel's hand.

Joey Jeter, screaming, turned around and kicked him and dumped a bottle of Pepsi over his head.

"You big drip! I'll get you for ripping my jacket!" he yelled.

Adam and Webb both punched Miguel in the back and the bigger guys knocked him down on the ground and one of them stepped on his leg. Then all of them ran off with Joey Jeter.

Miguel burst into tears. Oprah and Carla were hugging each other and sobbing. They ran over to help their brother who was crying harder than they had ever seen him cry.

"We're going to tell Mama!" Oprah said, grabbing her long braid and sticking it in her mouth to suck.

"And she'll tell their mamas," Carla said, sucking on her own black braid.

"No, no! You can't say nothing to her. Mama gets too mad. She will hit them and have to go to jail. And those guys will just beat me up more. You promise me not to say nothing, okay?"

6

The Return of Spring (ley)

The Monday after the baseball game, Miguel Rivera was slogging down the hall of Tortugas School, carrying his mother's old brown sweater. It had made him hot and itchy on the way to school. His mother made him wear it even though it wasn't even cold out. As he turned the corner on the way to his classroom, he spotted a long shadow on the hall floor. He looked up to see the outline of a very tall man in front of the window. The dazzling sunshine was pouring in all around him.

"Mr. Springley!" Miguel shouted. He galloped down the hall. "Mr. Springley! How ya doin', Mr. Springley!"

"Fine! How are you doing?" The sunshine made the highlights in the teacher's red hair crackle.

Miguel, filled with relief, was a helium balloon. "You're back!" he shouted. "Um . . . I didn't do much good work with Mrs. Cortés the . . . the Substitute, but I am sorry, Mr. Springley, I try. I . . ." Miguel sighed. He suddenly felt like crying.

He swallowed hard. He had too much pride to cry in front of Mr. Springley.

The teacher looked at Miguel without hurrying him. His attention did not waver. A little frown appeared above his left eyebrow. He was trying to get at the heart of what Miguel was saying. Miguel hoped the teacher did not notice the bruises on his cheek and on his chin from the fight Friday.

Something else was happening, too. Miguel was sure of it. Mr.

Springley, listening to him seriously, was more than a teacher. He was a . . . Miguel was scared to think of this. And then, just as suddenly he **wasn't** scared to think of it. Mr. Springley was his **friend,** as amazing and unexpected as that sounded. He himself was only eight, and Mr. Springley was a grown-up teacher. But he was a friend, too. Miguel felt heat pump into his cheeks.

It gave him the courage and trust to say, "Mr. Springley? Please. Can you give to me a desk in a different place? I don't like my seat."

Mr. Springley's eyelashes twitched. He looked as though he was figuring out a riddle or a puzzle.

Miguel was so astonished at his own nerve to ask the teacher for a change that he sputtered out, "Joey Jeter Cortés punches on me, and I couldn't say nothing . . . um . . . *any*thing." He took a breath. "To Mrs. Cortés, the Substitute. Did you *know* that she is *his* **mother***!*"

Mr. Springley grinned but was trying not to. He walked into the classroom where the other kids were taking their seats, chirping like birds. Their teacher was back. He opened his seating plan. He assigned Miguel a new seat.

It's not in front of anybody. It was the last seat in the second row, right behind Tim Blume, the new boy. Where Miguel wanted to be.

"Mr. Springley! Thank you. *Gracias! Muchas, muchas, muchas gracias!* Thank you!" he said so loud that he clapped his hand over his mouth when all the other kids stared at him. *How does Mr. Springley know Tim is my friend? My one and only friend in third grade?*

He sat at the new desk. It did not have even one initial carved into it. It smelled of furniture polish.

Miguel, taking a deep breath, relaxed, gazing at Mr. Springley, appreciating everything about him. He wore a sky blue sweater with a V neck. It looked new. His pants were khaki and his shoes, clean sneakers. He wore a big watch like an explorer's with all kinds of dials and gizmos. He noticed Mr. Springley's hand, too.

The teacher was wearing a shiny golden ring on his finger.

"Huh!" Miguel breathed out loud and then bent forward, whispering to Tim.

"You see that ring on his finger? It's new?"

Tim nodded. "What! Oh, no!" He whispered back, swiveling his head so that his wavy, light brown hair flopped over his smily face. "On **that** finger. Oh, no!"

"Maybe he married somebody?" Miguel whispered, feeling goose pimples rise on his arms.

Mr. Springley turned to the class. "Kids, I have news for you. I got me a little woman, as they said in the old days." He raised his left hand and flashed the ring at everybody in the class.

The pale, blond girl next to Miguel flushed red. She shouted, "Why didn't you tell us you were going to have a wedding, Mr. Springley! We thought you were dead."

Everybody gasped.

There was a terrible silence.

Mr. Springley's face turned fire-engine red, and then, sad.

"Yes!" Miguel added, "The Substitute didn't tell us nothing."

"It was private. That's why she didn't tell," Joey Jeter Cortés shouted in his ugliest voice. "I was the only one who knew. It was a secret, she said."

The class wiggled in their seats as if the chairs no longer fit them.

"Um . . . I didn't tell you, my friends, because I didn't know myself," Mr. Springley said in a low voice.

"What!" Webb and Adam said, sounding outraged.

"You did so know!" Webb said.

"No, I didn't know I was getting married. It was a surprise."

Everybody in the class looked horrified.

"We eloped. We didn't have a wedding or I would have invited every one of you. She asked me to marry her that Friday after school."

"She asked **you?**" two girls in front yelled.

"Yes. She said I was cute."

The kids screamed.

He said, "And since she was the first person who ever thought I was cute except for my mother . . . and what does she know, I was her only baby . . . I felt really grateful. So, I eloped with my wife as soon as we got a license. We needed a honeymoon, of course, so we took it. Got a plane to the Galapagos Islands to see the big sea turtles, I mean *tortugas*." Everybody was talking at once.

"What's your little woman look like, Mr. Springley?" a girl asked. "She pretty?"

"You'll see. She'll be here to pick me up in her car this afternoon. You can tell me what you think. In private, of course. If you think she's ugly, just whisper it. We wouldn't want to hurt her feelings. I'll introduce you. Stick around a few minutes if you can. She said she can't wait to meet my kids."

He sighed. It sounded as if he'd run the length of a basketball court without stopping. "Please sit down now, students. I am so darn sorry I worried you. I think I mistakenly thought somebody would tell you. It would have been all right, but I forgot to say it would be all right, so there's the confusion. Just a dumb mistake on my part. I wasn't thinking clearly."

The whole class sighed. Mr. Springley was very much alive. Everybody worked hard all day. Mr. Springley hardly had to teach or tell them what to do or scold anybody. The kids were like college students in third grade chairs.

Miguel looked around. *Nobody's doing nothing bad.*

"Gosh! Whooie! I forgot how smart you were," Mr. Springley said when they'd done the writing on their history assignment and finished ten whole minutes early. Miguel hated reading the history book. It was confusing. There were hardly any Mexicans. But even he got through it early like the rest of the kids.

At the end of the day, a few minutes before the last bell rang, there was a knock at the door. Everybody sat up straight. Miguel's heart was pounding.

"Here she is! My little woman," Mr. Springley said, blushing and throwing the door open wide. "Brooksie Rivers Springley. Brooksie was the woman's basketball champion at Texas Tech," he added.

Miguel didn't dare look at the other kids. He was scared he would laugh. Mr. Springley's "little woman" was over six feet tall. She was almost as broad shouldered as Mr. Springley himself. But walking through the door, she didn't have to duck like Mr. Springley.

"I never saw nothin' like her. She's the Statue of Liberty," Miguel whispered to Tim. He was sitting like a pole so he could see all of her. Tim was short in his seat, and on top of that he slid down so his neck rested easy against the top of the seat.

Mrs. Springley had platinum blond hair that flowed over her shoulders all the way down to her waist. Her eyes were robin's egg blue. She had dimples in her cheeks. When she smiled, everybody smiled right back. You couldn't help it!

The kids ran up front to meet her. They surrounded Mrs. Springley, full of happiness, full of chatter. Mr. Springley had come back to them. And he had told them why he was gone. He hadn't died. He hadn't abandoned them to Mrs. Cortés the Scary Stinky Substitute. He had just married a beautiful lady who thought he was cute and was brave enough to tell him so.

A woman could do that! It was all right, Miguel thought, wiggling his nose with surprise.

7

News

On December 6, Miguel was hurrying his sisters home. "Oprah! Carla! All us third grade kids, with . . . uh . . . with our families . . . I got it right! are invited to Mr. Springley's house. It's a party. New Year's Eve!"

"Is the house tall like him?" Carla said, her brown eyes wide, imagining what it would be like to go to a teacher's house.

Miguel nodded yes, because, although he didn't know, he wanted to sound as if he did. "If he lives in a flat-roof house, he can have the ceilings very high. Yes!"

"Do we meet the Statue of Liberty?" Oprah said, twisting her brown braid and sucking the tail of it.

Miguel giggled. "Sure do!"

"Thank you, Miguel, for asking us to your teacher's party! It's nice," Oprah said. She was polite.

"You're welcome. I'll be proud . . . to present you to my teacher. You talk so nice."

"You *introduce* me," Oprah said kindly.

"Oh . . ." He tried to get the right word to stick in his mind.

"I'll be nice, too!" Carla said, twisting her own long silky braid and powdering her nose with it.

"I know. I not afraid to introduce you to nobody either."

"To *anybody*," Oprah said gently.

"To anybody," Miguel said. "Right!"

Carla giggled. "Do you think that if the house is tall and the people living in it are tall, that the chairs are tall, too? And the sink? And the . . ."

"He told us they were. He did say so, yes."

"Then the toilet is high?" Carla said. She was short.

"Ssshhh! That's not polite," Oprah said.

"Go to the bathroom before you leave home," Miguel suggested, frowning.

There was a silence. Then he added, "But if you have to go *bad* at Mr. Springley's, you can climb up. But we won't say nothing, right?"

"*Anything*," Oprah and Carla chimed in together.

Miguel suddenly heard a whistle. He spun around and started yelling, "Run! Joey Jeter and his guys are coming! Hurry up!"

"Hey, wait up, Junk-i-canos!" Joey yelled down the street. "Got you a present."

Miguel started running, Oprah and Carla right behind him. Two blocks to go. Miguel snatched their hands and darted into the street. A UPS truck rumbled by. He made the girls duck down beside a dusty Ford Explorer parked at the curb while he posted himself lookout.

A police car was parked across the street, and the officer inside noticed the kids. He did not ask what they were doing. He did glance up and down the street.

When Miguel stuck his head up over the hood to check where the boys were, they had disappeared.

"Don't say nothing! This time we are lucky. They got tired of torture and maybe they saw the policeman. Joey Jeter can't get in trouble with the policeman because his dad's a border guard. He'd punish him if he did."

"Tell Mr. Sprinkle on those bad boys, Miguel. He can take them to the office," Oprah said.

"Springley. Not Sprinkle," Miguel said, giggling. Then, "I don't think it will save me to tell anybody."

When they got home, he felt safe for the first time since morning. Joey Jeter was getting meaner, not better. Tim Blume told

Miguel that he heard that Joey's gang had made up a secret name. They bragged that it was powerful and made them stronger.

So Miguel and Tim put their heads together and made up a name of their own for Joey's gang. They decided to keep it for ammunition in case they ever needed it. The name was a secret between them.

Miguel laughed when he thought of it, but he knew those mean guys would never get tired of torturing him.

He walked inside the apartment a few minutes later. It was perfumy with Mexican limes and bubbling chicken soup. It made his mouth water. Mama was calling him from the living room. He sensed excitement in her voice. Change was in the air for *la familia Rivera.*

8

Big News

Rosa and Crístobal Rivera, cuddling silent María Contenta between them on the sofa, said they had good news.

"What, Papa?" Oprah asked.

The twins climbed into their father's and mother's laps. Leaning over, they gave kisses to María who looked younger than they did. She made a little smile. It revealed a beautiful dimple in her cheek that they loved.

Rosa spoke softly. "Remember we ask God to help us a lot? Because we very poor. Right? Now we got an answer. I am so thankful." Rosa's eyes filled with tears and she had to take a deep breath before going on. "I not going to cry!" she promised. "*Es mucho bueno!* A man come here to the house. He give the chance to us to go to New México."

"When!" Miguel said all excited at the thought of a trip.

"When we will move there. He come from a store in Albuquerque, the biggest city in New Mexico. Is called México Fantastico Flea Market and Bargain House."

"Oh!" the children said, impressed.

"He is *Méxicano.* But no from Zacatecas, México. He come from Juárez across the river. Señor Fantastico. Yes! That's his name!" she said, laughing, her face bright again. "He want us to work in his store and sell the pillow covers and the pot holders we make. He want me to make the table covers and very beautiful bed covers and draperies for the windows. He say he will help us very much to find an apartment there."

"Wow!" Miguel said. Shivers ran up and down his spine because just this morning the voice in the bathroom's steamy mirror had said he was in for a surprise. He thought that the surprise was Mr. Springley's invitation to the party at his house. But this was even better than that.

"Is Albuquerque near Santa Fe?" he asked.

"Is no far . . . to Santa Fe," his father said.

"She can ski, Mama?"

"Well, maybe so. I see your mama get to taste the snow on a snow mountain."

"Gets to *ski*, Dad."

"Sure. But the work is first, Miguel. No one can say yes to the offer unless he and she can work. We will need much help, too."

"Do we have to move right away?"

"No, no, no! You go to the end of the third grade, Miguel. The girls will finish the nursery school," Crístobal said.

"We don't mess up your school. It is important," their mother said.

Miguel was relieved. "Oh! okay! I have to do a report on a big book. I don't want to read it. It's very hard. About all this stuff in Texas and New Mexico before I am born. Mr. Springley loves history. I don't like it, but Mr. Springley likes it. I'll read it to you, Mama. You can help me, okay?"

Rosa smiled. "I love you read me."

"I have to finish the book before we move away," he said. But he meant he couldn't leave Mr. Springley. Not until school was over and he had to go to a new teacher. Nobody was like this man. His good friend! Miguel wanted to tell his mother all these things. But she could only listen for a minute at a time. She was mostly at the sewing machine, whirring up the fabrics, biting the colored threads.

He sighed. To be moving away from his torturers. Away from Joey Jeter Cortés. *It is what I want, no?*

He wanted to tell Dad that. He wanted Dad to know Mr. Springley. Dad needed a friend, too. But he had no free time. He was working in the house all day. All night he was working in the auto parts lot, guarding it. His ears did not listen to no one. He was pale. Mama said all the time, "Cristobal! You too skinny! A little wind blow you away, and then what will we do?"

Mama rushed back to stir the *caldo de pollo* in the kitchen. The whole house smelled like chicken. Alone in the living room now, Dad bent over a low table, counting out bills. More dollars than Miguel, who looking longingly at him from the hall, had ever seen.

He ran into the living room. Startled, Dad swept the money into his pocket, his eyes flashing anger. He muttered in Spanish. It sounded like a curse. Miguel turned and ran out, his heart pounding, tears in his eyes.

Two minutes later, he peeked in again. Dad was slumped into an old armchair by the window. His hands covered his face and he was shaking. Miguel bit his lip. How could he go touch Dad's shoulder? How guess what to say . . . ?

Miguel didn't move. His lips formed Papa, but no breath carried the sound and worry out of his mouth.

He looked at his dad like he was a stranger. Like someone Miguel was trying to know, instead of somebody he knew already.

Cristobal Rivera was sleepy. His head dropped against the chair back. Sunshine from the window had fallen on his right shoulder and arm. Miguel thought it must be warming him. He noticed things. Papa's sneakers were worn out. His black jeans were ragged on the cuff. His gray sweater was ugly with holes. He had thin black hair and dry scarred hands. Without the smile on his face, Papa looked old.

Once he had been a soldier in Mexico. He got hurt shooting a rifle. It gave him a stiff shoulder. There were scars on his cheek and chin, too, from an explosion in a silver mine in Zacatecas. He had a sore ankle from falling off the garbage truck on the day after they crossed the border. Once he had told Miguel about his very first job—blowing glass in a factory at the age of nine.

"I liked that work," he said softly. "We made beautiful things."

Miguel wondered about Dad as a boy like him, going to work

at only nine, one year more than he, Miguel, had. No school for Dad. His parents couldn't give him shoes for school. They had no pesos for books.

Miguel turned his face away and swallowed. His heart, so happy a minute ago, felt heavy. He ran to the hall closet where he had left his lunchbox. Inside lay a chocolate devil's food cupcake wrapped in plastic. He had saved it from Tim's birthday party in school. Saved to eat in a private place where he could savor each soft sweet bite.

He stiffened his lip and ran the cupcake back down the hall. When he saw his father still sleeping, he tiptoed in. His mouth watered. It was hard to give up the cupcake, but he placed it gently on Dad's lap. He was snoring softly and didn't wake up.

Miguel ran into the kitchen and snitched a tortilla. He didn't dare look back at the cupcake.

9

First Trip to New Mexico

Early on the morning before Sunday, the twelfth of December, Rosa Rivera woke everybody up, shouting at the top of her voice.

"We going to the *fiesta* in Tortugas. A fiesta like in México. In the state of New México. I heard all about it at the laundromat. Tomorrow morning. I got the money here. I just counted it. We going!"

"Hush, Mom! I'm sleeping," Miguel whined, but curiosity dragged him right out of bed and plunked him on his feet. His cot was practically in the kitchen, where Rosa was slamming plates on the table.

"How we gonna get there? Fly?" her practical husband wanted to know. He plopped a cup and saucer on the table, and she grabbed the pot to pour him coffee.

"By bus, not even two hours. It leaves at 7:30. We be there before The Matachines dance. The people of Tortugas, they celebrate each year the mystery of *Nuestra Senora,* the Virgin of Guadalupe. How she appear to Juan Diego ... may God bless him and make him a saint! Bring hope for the poor people in México. And some of the rich who are not so bad, too. Miguel, it is history!" she said, splashing coffee all over Crístobal's saucer and the table. "We going to give many thanks to God. For all the gifts. For the work here in El Paso. For the new work in Albuquerque. For our secret IDs not being smelled by immigration police," she said, soaking up coffee with a sponge.

Miguel giggled. "Sniffed out, not smelled, Mom," he said.

"Oh, SNIFF? Like . . . like dog do . . . dogs do?"

Miguel burst out laughing.

"We have to give big thanks. **Big** thanks! Everybody in the family must do it," Rosa said, rolling out plans like a steamroller flattens bumps in a road.

"I work at night, remember, Rosa? I can't get off, " Miguel's father said in a cranky voice. "You can go for me."

"NO! We take the early bus. Be back in time for your work, Crístobal. You must go! Don't say NO! I be angry. Knock your block down."

Now Crístobal burst out laughing. "Rosita! Get it right. Knock your block OFF!"

Rosa giggled and raised her hands up in front of her. "I don't know what is a block? Miguel, tell me."

Crístobal gave her a hug and tapped her head gently with his fist, winking at the kids. "This is a BLOCK. And you got a hard one and a bossy one."

Everybody was laughing now. Even pale María Contenta smiled with joy. She was standing in her nightgown between the twins who were dressed for the day.

Rosa pointed a finger at Crístobal. "I pack a lunch and you will eat it, every bite! I going to ask God make you fat, and then, say the thanks for everything."

"Hey! I can't wait to go to New Mexico, Mama!" Miguel said. He'd been trying to get a word in over the noisy table. "I been looking at the New Mexico map Mr. Springley gave me. I love maps." He tapped his own head. "My block knows a lot, Dad."

His father gave him a weak smile.

"It could take a whole year to see all New Mexico. I gotta start if we're moving this summer."

Oprah said, "Mom! I don't know what to give a thanks for. Mama! Help me! I can't think of anything."

"Why not?" Miguel said, laughing. "You are a born citizen of United States of America."

"We going to give thanks for God help us with more money. We need it bad," Mama said, brushing Oprah aside. "Bad!"

"Can my friend Tim come with us?" Miguel said.

"Tim Blume? Of course! Nice boy. Polite. Intelligent. I see his mother at Tortugas School. She has blue-green eyes. I love them! She was the Peace Corps worker in Africa. She help poor people. Over there, they are really poor. More than **we** do, they know the smell of poor. The smell that make you sick. And scared." Rosa nodded her head. "When I get a little rich, I give to help them. Yes! I want Tim to come, too. I buy his ticket on the bus. I save for this. I have money. Plenty of it."

Miguel ran over to Tim's house to ask him. He wanted to tell him that they would get to see the Matachines Dance. It was done by men and a few young girls. When he was a little boy in Mexico, he had seen the Matachines. He remembered it because he had screamed. It scared him to death. Tim would like that. All the men and boy dancers wore spooky costumes and masks. One snapped a long skinny whip like a snake.

He knocked on the door of the only green house on Napoleon Street. An African bird carving stood on the mailbox. The wind was blowing so much dust up, the bird seemed to be moving. Miguel stared, wondering what its chirp was like. He liked birds.

The door opened a crack.

Tim peered out, but he did not let Miguel in. He was in pajamas.

"Are you sick?" Miguel said.

Tim shook his head, but he looked odd.

Miguel said, "Tomorrow we're going to Tortugas, a little town in New Mexico near Las Cruces. (He had already looked and found it on his map.) For the Matachines Dance. We want to invite you to come. Mom will buy your ticket!"

Tim looked sad and whispered, "I can't come out today, buddy. I can't let you in either. And my Dad's coming tomorrow to take me to a museum."

"Aww . . ." Miguel sighed. "Wish you could go."

"Joey Jeter and his gang followed me home yesterday afternoon.

I yelled, '**Leave Me Alone!**' They didn't. So I told 'em, '**Miguel and I don't like you.**' I didn't say, you're stinkers. But I did say, '**we hate your guts.**'"

"Out loud?" Miguel said, eyes wide.

Tim shook his head no, but he said yes. "I spit at 'em, too. I said Miguel and I found out your secret gang name. They said what? So I said, '**The Big Poops.**'"

"You didn't say **that?** Now they will kill us."

"Right!" he said nervously. " 'We'll kick you around like soccer balls next time we see you,' they said. That's when they hit me. Made bumps and bruises on my head." He rubbed his purple cheek. His blue eyes had shadows under them and he didn't look so good.

"Now my mother's scared," Tim went on, "all upset and sad, too. She says I have to learn how to make peace. She's teaching me words . . . a peace vocabulary. Says everybody should learn it." He rolled his eyes. "*Guts* and *poop* and some other words I can't say aren't in it. I have to learn it today. She won't let me do nothing else."

"*Anything else,*" Miguel said, proud to correct somebody else's English. Mr. Springley was drilling him on correct speech in "Private Time" at school. Each kid got five minutes of his private attention. It happened Thursdays.

"I only say that word *nothing* because that is what you say, Miguel!" Tim yelled back, laughing as if nothing was the matter. "What is the Machines you're talking about? What kind of machines? Machines don't dance."

"A dance called *Mat-a-**chi** -nes*. Chee chee chee. I seen it in Mexico. They do it in New Mexico, too. Mama wants to see if they do it right."

"Will she know that? Doin' it right?"

"Doing it . . ."

"Yeah."

"Yes! She was one of the *malinches,* ma-lin-ches, when she was little. The good little brides. Her father was the *General Azteca*

Chichimeca for the Virgin of Guadalupe procession."

"Wow!" Tim said, mystified. "Can you take pictures and show me?"

"No. We don't have no camera."

"I don't have *a* camera," Tim said, correcting Miguel.

"Oh! *A* camera."

"But I do," Tim said. "It has film in it. I can lend it to you."

"Timothy! The wind's blowin' the dust in! Close the door, Sweetie," Mrs. Blume called from inside the house. Her voice was like a song.

"Okay, Mom! Just wait here, Miguel. I'll close the door, but I'll bring it to you."

"Okay!"

After Tim gave him the camera, Miguel said thanks. He was thrilled to have a camera to use. He ran home fast as if The Big Poops were hot on his trail.

10

An Amazing Invitation

Miguel called Mr. Springley to accept the invitation for the New Year's Party. Miguel was so nervous the telephone receiver almost escaped his sweaty hand.

Mr. Springley sounded like he did in person, calm with excitement ready to burst out. "So," he said. "All of you Riveras are coming over to our house on New Year's Eve? Right?"

"Right! Me, my three sisters, Mom, and Papa . . . Dad. Six of us!"

"I can't wait to meet them. Everybody's going to eat lasagna and milk shakes. Brooksie makes 'em. Wear comfortable clothes. We're going to play charades," the teacher said.

"Oh!" Miguel said, his mind as blank as new paper at the word *charades*. "Guess what, Mr. Springley?"

"What?"

"We going to New Mexico tomorrow. To Tortugas. The town. Same name as your school. Mom and Dad have to visit a chapel there tomorrow. Then see the Matachinas Dance, famous in Mexico. My mother was in the dance when she was little."

"That dance *is* famous in New Mexico and very old. But sorry to say, I've never seen it."

"Oh!" Miguel said, inspired. "Would you like to come with us? We are taking the morning bus."

"I've always wanted to see it. Hey!" Sounding excited now, Mr. Springley said, "What if I drive you all there? I have a van. Holds nine. Plenty of room! Maybe my little woman can come, too. I'll ask her."

Miguel was surprised at the offer. And he was surprised that Mr. Springley wanted to see the dance. But he was most surprised that he wanted to be with him and his family. Miguel swallowed. He did not know what to say. He wished Mom were on the phone, not he, himself. Nothing came out of his mouth.

"Miguel? There's a problem," the teacher said. "We have to be back for a party. Eight o'clock. So I'd have to leave Tortugas by five."

Miguel caught his breath. "My dad has to come home, too. He's a security guard at night. He eats dinner and has a little sleep first."

"Go ask your mom if it's all right with her for me to drive. She can tell me all about the Matachinas Dance."

"I'm going to take pictures with Tim's camera."

"Great! Give a report to the class and get extra credit. You need some good grades to bring up your report card."

Miguel, holding the receiver tightly, shook his head. "I'm a little bit scared," he said real low.

"Of what?"

It had to do with being an illegal immigrant, of course. Dad said Immigration and Naturalization Service authorities were known to come to fiestas related to the country of Mexico. Border patrolmen came looking for people who live scared of being discovered without the right papers. They had to be careful and not make any mistakes. Miguel wondered if that was why his father had been so very troubled by the money he was counting in the living room yesterday. Was it illegal? Miguel was afraid to even think of it, let alone ask.

If he gave a report about the Matachines Dance, Joey Jeter would tell his mother, the scary substitute, or his father, Sergeant Cortés, the border patrolman.

"Scared of what?" Mr. Springley repeated over the telephone. "You can tell me, Miguel! I keep secrets like money. Safe."

Miguel said, "I have to ask Mom about riding in your van. You sure you want to go?"

"I do."

"I can call you back, okay? Thank you very much," he added and hung up.

11

FIESTA!

"Look at them! **Here** is my México!" Rosa Rivera cried, bursting into happy tears and hugging her son.

"Let me go! I can't breathe," Miguel said, laughing. She had such a tight hug.

Rosa had reached the dirt plaza in front of the Tortugas church dedicated to the Virgin of Guadalupe. "I so happy, everybody! My little heart so grateful!" she said as though through a microphone.

Miguel cringed. Americans were cool and careful, he thought, while his mother was firecrackers. One day she might become an American naturalized citizen—her big hope—but her heart would always be red hot, like her colorful, gorgeous native country. Everybody in the family knew she missed it terribly. But today? She got it all back.

"Thank you, Mr. Springley, for bring us in your van."

"Thank you, Mrs. Rivera, for letting me," Mr. Springley said, blushing at the compliment that he had had a little something to do with Miguel's mother's wonderful happiness. He was still a young man. He loved to see anybody glad, especially a student. But Miguel's mother was a fountain of joy. Mrs. Rivera over-whelmed him. It was as if he had met the First Lady. He was awestruck.

And Rosa Rivera looked sensational in a beautiful dress embroidered with gold, red, and blue threads. The tears caused by her exuberance sparkled like diamonds in the corners of her eyes.

The teacher knew from meeting her why Miguel was such a brilliant boy. He was his mother's child, sensitive, kind, and full of life. Mr. Springley thought that Miguel felt about things a little like he, himself, did. They were, as the *Méxicanos* said of special friendships, *simpático.*

A Matachine dancer at the fiesta in Tortugas, New Mexico, was shaking rattles and clackers, and shifting back and forth across the ground. Guitars were playing. It was grand. It was wild. The costumes, strange and mysterious.

Stopping himself from shivering with excitement, Miguel snapped a photograph of a line of masked men dancers. "The clackers look like bows and arrows, don't they?" he whispered to Dad and Mr. Springley.

His father nodded, but his attention was elsewhere. He was looking over the huge crowd carefully. The Rivera family, dressed finely, had just pushed into the crowd on the plaza. They stood to the left of the church with its high white steeple and simple form.

"Look at the dancers in Indian headdresses! Their scarves cover their faces. The ribbons hang down like the tails of shooting stars," Mr. Springley said.

"*Los Matachines!* The guitars! *Las malinches,* the sweet girls!" Rosa said, twirling her white skirts as she watched, moving her feet and hands and dancing a little, too.

"The men dancers are spooky," Miguel whispered.

"No doubt about it! They are," Mr. Springley said. On the drive to Tortugas, Rosa had told the story of the Virgin of Guadalupe, how in the winter long long ago, the Virgin of Guadalupe told Juan Diego, a Mexican Indian, he would find red roses on the top of a mountain where they never grew.

"He needed the miraculous flowers for a token to show the Spanish bishop. He did not believe the Virgin would appear to a poor Indian like Juan Diego. But when he carried them inside, the flowers proved to the bishop that he had seen the Virgin. A lasting miracle for the Mexicans!

"The Virgin of Guadalupe herself looked just like an Indian,"

Mr. Springley with deep respect would say for all the rest of the years he taught.

Rosa said, "Mr. Springley, I hang the pictures of the Virgin in her starry blue cape in many places. Near my sewing machine, near my stove, the refrigerator, and near the kids. She give *muchas muchas muchas* protection."

Miguel cringed, wishing she hadn't said *muchas muchas muchas*. He wanted her to just use English in front of Mr. Springley. He had told her so this morning. But did she listen to him?

"My Brooksie would have been knocked out by the costumes!" Mr. Springley said.

"What a shame she miss it!" Rosa said, patting his arm. "But next year we bring her, and I take very appropriate care of the baby while Mrs. Springley look at everything, okay?"

"Okay," Mr. Springley said, blushing. He had told them a secret about Mrs. Springley. Brooksie had not come because she was sick to her stomach.

Why was she sick? She was pregnant. The Riveras promised not to tell this sweet secret because Rosa said, "Don't tell everybody, Mr. Springley! Babies are safer if they appear as a surprise. Like a sunrise. You know the sun is coming every morning, no? But it is a surprise every time, no? You feel the warmth of the Creator on to your skin, the most warmly of all our spirits."

Mr. Springley nodded, not even wanting to correct Miguel's mother's English because of its poetry. Miguel was quietly gloating over the fact that he knew the secret before Joey Jeter did. Not even if he tortured him would Joey Jeter get the precious secret from him. He half wished that Joey Jeter would try.

But maybe he could whisper it to Tim Blume, who would never say "poop" or "guts" again or probably tell secrets because of the peace vocabulary he was learning. Tim he could trust. Yes!

Mr. Springley said to Crístobal and Miguel, "After the Mexican War this little town in the Mesilla Valley was settled. It attracts a world of people."

"Lots of Mexicans are here today. I see American Indians and Anglos, too," Miguel replied.

"Right! All kinds. *E pluribus unum.* That's our country's motto. Out of many, one," Mr. Springley said. He bent down to Oprah, Carla, and María Contenta. "The Matachines Dance came to New Mexico with early Spanish settlers and their ideas. Some of their ideas were damaging maybe, but a lot were really helpful."

The girls were hugging each other they were so enthralled by the sights. They blinked and giggled, dazzled by the teacher's height and bright red hair. Their father was like a neat robin, Mr. Springley like a flapping red crow.

Some male dancers wore aprons with pictures of Our Lady of Guadalupe on them. The women's Pueblo Indian dresses had a black strap over one shoulder. Girls of Miguel's age wore white dresses made of delicate lace. They were pretend brides looking radiant and shy, too.

"They represent purity and goodness. I studied this before I came," Mr. Springley said.

"Mama! I want to be in the dance and wear a pretty dress!" Oprah cried. "Mama! Please!"

"You'd be pretty," Mr. Springley said.

"Of course, Oprah. One day all three of you girls will be in the dance. I will make the gorgeous costumes," their mother said.

Their father's mouth was a tight line as if he were engaged in a battle of good and evil, like the dance expressed.

Miguel noticed that General Azteca Chichimeca wore a mountain of feathers on his head. His apron was made of reeds that rattled. Everyone looked dead serious. The masked men pretended to fight among one another. Oddly, one of them seemed to be looking at the Riveras. The sight brought tears to Rosa's eyes. It made her so terribly homesick, she felt queasy and lost.

The little Rivera girls were shaking. Miguel took their pictures huddling behind their mother and father. The man wearing the horrifying, ugly mask of the *Abuelo*, the cruel grandfather, came near and cracked his whip. They screamed. Oprah, Carla, and María

Contenta, told it was a play and not real life, giggled nervously.

"Look how people from every place come together in one dance! It makes friends of strangers. Friends of enemies. *E pluribus unum*," Mr. Springley said again to Miguel's father. "Miguel! You can learn history this way."

Miguel wrinkled his nose. Mr. Springley pumped him on the back. "Someday you'll like it. It's fun to know things."

"Crístobal, *mi esposo!*" Rosa said urgently. "Come into the chapel now. It is time." Hugging shy María Contenta to her side, Rosa cooed to her, "María! Come look. Inside the church is pretty flowers and the candles on fire. It smell so nice."

Overhead helicopter blades whirred. Miguel looked up.

"It's them!" his dad muttered to him.

"Oh, Dad!" he said sadly. How different were the moods today of his mother and father.

The Immigration Service was flying over Tortugas. The sounds thundered in the hearts of Rosa and Crístobal. They looked at one another anxiously. Miguel saw a worry line appear in his teacher's smooth face.

When the family went toward the church to offer their prayers, Mr. Springley said, "I'll come back in half an hour." It was sunny. He loved watching people. He didn't want to interrupt or bother them in any way. "Please take your time. Stay longer if you need to," he said kindly.

Miguel saw the teacher trying to be friendly to Papa. Yet his father's face was as closed as a trap. Miguel wondered if he even really saw the wonderful teacher. In the van the two men, sitting up front together, had talked to each other. Leaning forward over the back of his dad's seat, Miguel had tried to add bits of his own thoughts to the conversation. Most of the talk, though, had come from his gentle and considerate teacher.

Early this morning Miguel had stood up in the hot bathtub to ask the steamy face in the mirror to let Mr. Springley become his father's friend. The face had laughed. Actually! After all the helpful things, it had turned mean.

Miguel, angry, swore he'd never speak to it again. *I don't need that slime, the spirit of fog. It's not real anyway.* He couldn't admit to himself how its nasty new attitude scared him.

In their prayers of thanksgiving, each Rivera child had been directed to mention five good things. Miguel's started with Timothy Blume, and then the big white bathtub, and, of course, his Mr. Springley.

Mama lit a candle in a red glass holder for each member of the family. Each one cost a dollar contribution. María Contenta, kneeling at the altar filled with roses, put her hands over her face and whispered something but nobody heard what it was.

The chapel was full of people praying. Some knelt down at the door and crawled down the aisle on their knees, their faces glowing with the effort it took and the pain. Mom smiled at Miguel like an angel in the candlelight. He then thanked God for two more things: Mama in her best embroidered dress and the sewing machine. You could mention a whole lot of things for a dollar. It didn't cost any more, she said.

When they went outside again into the bright sunshine, Mr. Springley was there with another man, talking. Seeing Miguel and his family, the teacher's face lit up.

"Here they are!" he said to the man, who spun around quickly and glared at Miguel's dad. The man, in pressed jeans and white shirt, was fit. He had a black, nipped mustache and tightly cropped hair.

"Miguel! Crístobal! Rosa! Girls!" Mr. Springley said happily. "Look who I ran into. Another student's parent. Meet Joey Jeter's dad. Sergeant Richard Cortés! He danced in the Matachines dance. Didn't you?"

"For a little bit," Sergeant Cortés said, his chin raised. "I just wanted to try it."

"I thought you had to be a member of the dancers' group," Mr. Springley said.

"They let me in," he said as if it weren't something special, when everyone knew it was.

12

Something Wrong

Fear shot through Miguel. He looked over at Dad, his face as hard as a rock scraped and scalded by wind and sun.

Miguel, holding María Contenta's hand, suddenly grabbed her around the waist. She let out an ear-piercing wail. He knew she would cry out because she was always scared. Lifting her a few inches off the ground, he carried her awkwardly to Dad.

Crístobal bent over and scooped the poor little girl into his arms. All this happened in the flick of an eye. Nobody had spoken yet to Sergeant Cortés except for Mama. She rushed over with Oprah and Carla and shook his hand.

"These are my twins. Oprah and Carla. Born in Texas," she said. "Like Miguel."

"What! What!" María, the silent, screamed loud enough that passersby stopped to check what was wrong.

"Daddy! She's upset. Hold her tight!" Oprah said.

Sergeant Cortés's eyes narrowed. Looking strained, suspicious, and irked, he suddenly was saying, "Got to be going. Good-bye!"

Mr. Springley, who always had words to say, merely shook his head. He was mystified.

"Oh, wait! Miguel, take a photo of Sergeant Cortés. You can show it to his *hijito*, his boy, when the pictures get done," Rosa said in her strong voice.

Sergeant Cortés raised his hand. "No, no. No thanks. Good-bye."

That night, after they returned home to El Paso, Crístobal Rivera was leaving the apartment early to go to work. Miguel ran to him and threw his arms around his waist.

"Dad, don't go yet! I liked our trip together. It was fun."

His father stopped, looked down at Miguel and sighed. His shiny brown eyes turned soft. "I am so sorry I don't have the time to play ball with you. Or the time to take you places. But one day, I will have the time. When things go good in Albuquerque, I will not need the work at night. I stay home then, Miguel, watch TV with you."

"Good, Dad!"

"And one day very soon I take you into the mountains, where we will sleep under the stars like the trees do."

Miguel caught his breath. He had always wanted to camp out at night.

"I promise. Just you and me. We can walk in wild places."

"Will we be scared?" Miguel asked.

"No. Wild places is good. In the wild places, I think you and I will know the good that was put in our hearts when we were born." He sighed. "Sometimes I feel like a criminal. But I had no choices. So I get the fake ID papers so we can come here to work." He looked sad but then smiled again. "In the wild places we will be free to make friends with the bears." Crístobal grinned at Miguel, his eyes twinkling. "You won't be scared, will you?"

"Not if you're there."

At that, his father's eyes lit up. "Ah! You know it. I will always be there with you, *hijito*. Always. My father say he is always with me. He is in my heart. Very strong." He struck his chest hard three times with his open palm. "Here, just here, my papa. Bye, now, son."

The front door opened and closed quickly. Everything Dad did was fast and neat. No extra fussiness. Miguel wished he could camp out with Dad right away. He needed him. Of all the people in the world, he wanted to be *his* friend most. He stood there thinking. Then he noticed a medium-sized paper bag on the cardboard box near the door. They used the box as a little table. He looked inside the bag to be sure it was what he thought it was. Dad's sandwich and apple lay on a paper towel, a can of soda on top. He stuck his hand in further. The bag seemed too big for the contents, and Miguel discovered money on the bottom. A lot of bills. He quickly closed the bag.

Then it hit him. He'd sneak out, bring the bag with him, and help Dad in the car parts plant. It was only a mile or so. He knew the way.

"Goin' to bed, Mom!" he yelled down the hall.

"See you in the morning!" she said loudly over the whirr of the stitching needle on her machine. "I like your Mr. Springley. He so good to us. And what a nice car!"

"I be a teacher like him someday," he said, wiggling into his Windbreaker.

"Good! Go to bed. Don't wake the girls. They asleep already."

At the door to the apartment, he hit himself hard on the chest three times and silently let himself out.

13

Smugglers

Miguel tiptoed down the musty stairway. The dust was heavy on the wooden steps. It smelled of garbage rotting in the trash barrels. It smelled of sadness, because Mr. Iturbide, the custodian, was nursing his dying wife and could only do some of his work. Rosa had taken to washing the hall floor on the third floor to help Mr. Iturbide out. Miguel had hauled the trash for the whole building to the curb on the last two Thursdays.

Downstairs he laid his palms flat against the cool panes of the front door. He did not feel afraid though it was dark and he had never been alone after sunset. When he pulled the heavy varnished door open, the night rushed in around him.

"Whoo!" he cried like an owl to scare off any critters that might be waiting. He stepped out, his father's paper bag zipped inside his jacket. At the end of the block a streetlight glowed. He ran to it as fast as he could go. Not a person on the street. No cars moving. The quiet was empty.

He breathed in and let the air whistle through his lips. He put his hand on a light pole, liking its firmness. He had his destination firmly in mind. His feet tingled.

Now which way?

Toward town, he said out loud, as if he were a traffic cop giving directions. He had to cross, so checking for cars, he ran like a flash over the road. Then, because it felt good, he kept running all the way down the block and over to the next street. It was the main avenue leading to the parts factory. "Dad takes fifteen minutes to get there," he said.

Then I can make it in twenty.

"I can't wait to see him," Miguel said, as if somebody were listening. He took another breath and kept running. A truck rumbled past on the other side. He didn't like this big street as much as the little ones. It was wider and better lit but it made him feel small. It made him easy to see, too. And this was a private trip. *I don't want nobody askin' questions.* He ran so fast he got a stitch in his side and had to stop.

Glancing in the dusty window of a hospital supply store, he saw crutches and wheelchairs. He turned his head away and ran another block of small houses on either side. He passed Jim's Saloon. It was stinky. Country music plunk, plunk, plunking filled his ears.

A man leaning against the wall asked him for money.

"Next time. Sorry," Miguel said.

Miguel decided to get off this street and turned the corner. He expected to see the sign of the car parts factory ahead. But he wasn't where he thought he was. He ran three more blocks before he finally saw the neon orange and red sign for the big plant.

PARTS! *FOR* **ANY CAR or ANY TRUCK!**

He stopped to catch a breath. Happy. A light was flipped on inside his heart, guiding him. That's how good he felt.

It led him to the place he knew. He didn't get lost. He smiled and exhaled with a little roar. He was so proud of himself alone at nighttime.

An eight-foot chain-link fence surrounded the parts plant. Only one light was blazing in the yard. It was near the brick building's door. He wanted to get closer to it, closer to Dad, who was not in sight. Miguel was scared to call to him. It seemed wrong to do. He reached the gate that was the entrance to the yard and found it unlocked.

That stopped him. Made him wonder. He pulled on the heavy iron gate so he could slip inside. At that very moment, he heard shouts coming from the yard. Spanish shouts, Mexican voices. They were furious. He turned and ran out.

Then there was a cry of pain and moans. He thought he heard fists pounding someone's body. He gasped, wondering if he should run all the way home. Get his mother. Two men came racing out of the small storage unit near the light. That was where his dad kept his thermos of coffee. The heavy-set men in sweatshirts and black baseball caps came running toward Miguel and the gate. Miguel ducked behind a trash can and squeezed himself small and invisible. He closed his eyes. He waited for them to storm past, running like the wind. They threw open the gate and left it wide open. Miguel opened his eyes and saw their angry faces. Sick with dread, he flew into the lot again. He ran around the piles of boxes and wooden crates to find Dad. He reached the storage house and pushed inside.

Cristobal Rivera lay on the floor moaning, his face bloody and his hands tied behind him. Miguel burst into tears and sank on the greasy floor beside him. "Dad! Dad! Say something to me. Please!"

"Miguel? You. Here? Am I in heaven?"

"No, Dad, I'm here. I . . . I came to help you. What happened?" He worked to unknot and rip off the rope twisted around his father's wrists. "Who were those guys?"

"We have to lock the gate. I let them in. They made me. Go lock the gate fast," he said breathlessly.

Miguel flew to the gate, locked it tight and hurried back.

Cristobal said, "They are *Méxicanos*. Been here before. Get me in trouble. They tell me to let six workers inside the yard to hide here. They smuggle workers from Mexico, to be picked up here by somebody I don't know who."

"Take it easy, Papa! Take a breath."

" I can't let the workers in. I lose my job. I let down Mr. DeFord, the owner."

"Dad, you have to go to the hospital."

"No. I can't. They find me out and arrest me. Deport me." He pushed himself up, stumbling and bleeding. "Does your mother know you're here, son?"

"Thinks I'm asleep," Miguel said, only half afraid Dad would scold.

"I have some money from those men. I was going to give it back to them. I don't want that money but I forgot to bring it," he mumbled. "It's death money." Crístobal stumbled across the yard back to a wooden crate where he leaned his back gingerly against a rough wall. "We need more lights here. The criminals would not come and bother me if the lot had real bright lights. I will tell Mr. DeFord. No. I can't tell him. He would be made suspicious. He would not trust me again. Those criminals from my country want me to help them smuggle poor people from Mexico. It's evil. The poor people die in the hot trucks they carry them in. They are not like the Amigas who we paid to help us cross the border when you were a little boy."

He put his head into his hands and moaned.

Miguel said softly, "Here's your lunch bag. You left it by your chair at home."

14

A Scary Change

When the faithful sun came up, Miguel and his father walked home together. Crístobal Rivera was limping, aching and bloody. He was telling Miguel the many, many things he worried about.

"If *la migra* pick me up for not having good papers, I be deported. If they find me with bribe money, they deport me. If somebody stick drugs in my pockets even though I don't use, don't sell it, they deport me."

"Back to Mexico, is that it?"

"Your mother have to take care of everything, make all the money for the family."

"I won't let this happen, Dad. I can help. I can think about what to do. But you need to wash off yourself, Dad. Okay?"

They reached the apartment before anyone was awake inside. Miguel ran the water in the tub and his father sank into it, moaning. He washed himself all over.

Miguel sneaked down the hall to tell Mama, who slept on an air mattress in the living room, what had happened to Dad. He told her before she was quite awake so that she would not burst out in anger at his sneaking out at night.

Instead of yelling, Rosa surprised him by pulling him close to her.

"You are wonderful, Miguel. The best boy I ever know. To think you are my own! Thank you! I am so glad that like a man, Miguel, you help your *papacito*," she said.

Miguel was so happy she said that.

Rosa got up and went into the bathroom to put salves and bandages on Crístobal's hurts. She was as gentle with him as with María Contenta. And she did everything quietly, cooing like a lovebird over him.

Miguel stood to one side of her, exhausted and sad.

"Crístobal, I want you to take the bus and go to Albuquerque to see that man who wants us to come and to work there. I want you to go right away. This morning. Now before anything else happens," Rosa said. "I will take care of the family and the work here, but you must leave. Quickly. Now."

"But he'll miss Mr. Springley's New Year's party if he has to go," Miguel said.

"Ssh!" his mother said, her eyes like a fierce lioness's suddenly.

Miguel ran out of the bathroom and down the hall. He crawled into his cot and cried.

15

Good-byes

After calling the owner of the auto-parts plant and telling him that he had to leave El Paso without delay, Crístobal Rivera said good-bye to everyone in his family. His little daughters stared at him and did not say anything. María Contenta was clinging to his arm and scarcely breathing.

Miguel wondered if they understood what *going away* really meant.

But María Contenta must have understood the meaning of leaving, because when Crístobal kissed her good-bye she burst into anguished tears. It was the thing that made the moment of good-bye so terrible. After he put her down on a kitchen chair, María Contenta went on patting her own arms crossed tightly across her chest.

Crístobal's face was swollen, cut and bruised. The sharp Texas light showed every mark. Rosa walked him to the apartment door by herself, forbidding anyone to go with them. The kids in the kitchen could hear their whispers. They did not talk, only listened. Then the door went *chaclumpbum*. They heard their mother sobbing. Nobody went to school that day.

In the middle of the following week, Rosa asked Miguel to help her with cutting out shapes for her pot holders. They were designed to look like chiles, apples, avocados, and limes. He liked laying out the patterns on the cloth but he botched the cutting.

They had to throw away eleven pieces of fabric, and that made her scold him.

After Crístobal left for Albuquerque with his clothing, carving knife, and fake citizenship papers, Rosa Rivera became even stronger, her voice louder. Miguel did not understand that her powerful voice made her feel safer in the hard world. She was strict and bossy, and Miguel couldn't wait until he was with Dad again.

"You don't have to talk to me so loud, Mom. Can I tell you a memory trick Mr. Springley taught us today?" He stopped trying to cut the patterns out and his mother nodded. "He gave us a list of words. They didn't have nothing to do with each other. Mine were:

hungry,
beach,
turquoise,
taxicab,
banana,
seat,
heavy,
dog,
window,
dollar,
doctor,
left over,

and needle. He said if you made up a story using the words, you could remember all of the words in order."

Rosa said, "You good at stories?"

He nodded.

"What did you make up?"

"A story." As he told it, Miguel put up one of his fingers each time he hit a word Mr. Springley had given him. "A *hungry* man went to the *beach*. A *turquoise taxicab* went by. The driver had three *bananas* on the *seat* that were spoiling in the sun. A *heavy dog* smooshed them. She threw them out the car *window* to the starving man. He ate one. He sold the rest *left over* for a *dollar* to a *doctor*. The doctor practiced giving shots by sticking a *needle* in the bananas."

Rosa roared with laughter. "That's a big story! I can understand why it help you remember the words. Is good way!"

"I was best in the class. I was, Mom! I was. I could do twenty words at a time. Mr. Springley says I am smart, but not good in homework. Joey Jeter tells me I am not smart, but dumb as a dumb cluck."

"What?"

He shrugged. "I don't know. He says he's going to beat me up. But . . ." Miguel's eyes lit up and he giggled. "But this time I say something back. I get him," Miguel giggled.

"What did you say?" Rosa said, running her soft hand down his cheek and tweeking his earlobe.

"I say my mother, Rosa Rivera, knows your father. And if you touch me, she will beat him up!"

Rosa sighed and shook her head. "No, no, Miguel. Is no chance. His father and another officer—a very tall man with the eyebrows big and hairy and a mad voice—knock at my door this morning."

"What!" Miguel said.

"Yes. Sergeant Cortés say very loud he want to see my husband. I say, my husband not in the house. He say, I come back tomorrow. I say, he not here tomorrow. Gone. Where? he say, a bad mood in his voice. I do not know what to say now, so I say to Sergeant Cortés, I do not know. Sorry."

"Oh, no!" Miguel said.

"He seemed very suspicious and angry. I say to him, my husband is tired from too much work. I say, he did not tell me what you want to know. I also say, I trust him for he is a very good man. Like Jesus. Very kind. I say the last loud because I am feeling angry and fear. Then I remember the secret money and am afraid this man will search my house. If he find the money here, he put me in jail. Just because of that evil money Crístobal wanted to give back to the smugglers that time."

Miguel and Rosa looked at one another.

"Mom, why did the men come here?" Miguel said, heart

pounding.

"To see your father, I said. I glad he leave El Paso two days ago."

"But what did Sergeant Cortés want?"

"I don't know. He ask, do you pay taxes? I say, yes I do. Just call the IRS and Texas Tax and Revenue people. They know me very well," her voice weak for a change. I tell Crístobal not to telephone me in case the agents try to trace the call. I don't know what to do now, Miguel. I just a little bit scared all by myself now."

Miguel stood up and said, "I'm here, Mama. You're not alone."

That night Rosa Rivera let the air out of her mattress and started packing the house. She did not tell Miguel, who awakened when he heard her rummaging in the kitchen for her special plastic woven bags. A good friend had brought them from Mexico. They would be her suitcases.

"Go back to sleep for now," she said gently. "Sleep well, my little son, for tomorrow's coming soon."

Part Two

MIGUEL RIVERA
IN A NEW WORLD

1

Dinner in a New World

Miguel Rivera, now ten years old, was nervous. Something smelled funny. He pulled out a carved chair from the long polished table, dusted off his pants, and sank into a velvety cushion. He looked around quickly to see everything before his friend came back to the dining room. Black and red Navajo rugs lay scattered on the floor. Big dusty Indian pots rested on tops of cabinets near its beamed ceiling. Through the window Albuquerque's huge Sandia Mountains glowed in the red, hot sunset.

The kitchen door swung open. Albert King ran through and held the door for his father and grown-up brother. "Here's Miguel, Pop!" he said. Albert was good looking with skitter-skatter blond hair and eyes the color of sky. The first time they met he said, "Guess what? I'm kin to a New Mexico governor named King."

Was he or wasn't he?

"Hi there! Welcome, Miguel!" said Mr. King, a big, beaming, handsome man. He came right over to shake hands like Miguel was a man, too.

"Hello, Mr. King! Thank you for having me to dinner here." Miguel had never eaten in a friend's home before. He had never been in a family dining room before either. His family ate in the kitchen. He might do something stupid or impolite. That worry killed his appetite.

Mr. King held a platter in his other hand. "Leg of lamb tonight, Miguel. Like it rare? That's how we eat it." He took off his cowboy hat and tossed it on an empty chair. Mr. King was too pale to be a cowboy or a rancher, Miguel thought. He had a straight nose, a strong chin, and wore a handsome white shirt, a woven vest, and carved leather boots.

"Sure, I like it rare, Mr. King," Miguel answered, but he'd never tasted lamb. Up until now he didn't even know people ate baby sheep.

Mr. King loaded Miguel's plate with meat. It was bloody. The saliva thickened in his mouth and he swallowed. *It's not dead yet?*

Mr. King's handsome son, Bucky, twenty-one, who had muscles and glossy black curly hair, filled the glasses with iced tea. Then he plopped green jelly on Miguel's plate next to the meat. "Mint jelly, great with lamb," Bucky said.

Jelly with meat? Weird! Why don't Bucky and Albert look alike? Why don't kids in the U.S. match the other kids in their families? They have a rainbow of colors for eyes and hair. It's weird, too, like eating jelly with meat.

The thought of that green jelly made Miguel want to giggle. What was it made from? Leaves? Albert's brother clapped a heavy hand on Miguel's shoulder and said. "How's it goin'?"

"Okay. How's it goin' for you, Bucky?" Miguel said, his face heating up because of all the attention.

"Got a new chef's job. At Rainbows. Everybody comes. It's a blast. Want some tortillas?" As he sat down at the place across from Miguel, his shoulders blocked half the view from the window.

"Okay, thanks," Miguel said, laying his white cloth napkin across his lap like Albert did.

"I made tortillas just for you. It's your staff of life, right?" He looked at Albert for confirmation that Miguel was indeed Mexican.

Miguel hoped Bucky wasn't mocking his being *Méxicano*. He was very sensitive about it. He lifted the napkin off the basket and took two tortillas off the stack. It turned out they were fragrant and warm just like his mother's, and easy to eat.

"Pop, bad news!" Albert said. "We lost our game today. Even though I made a double play and Miguel hit a homer."

Mr. King and Bucky praised them both, but Miguel shrugged. All he cared about was winning. He took a bite of the meat and some potato.

"I rubbed the lamb with garlic and rosemary like we do at the café. That's what you smell," Bucky said, neatly slicing his meat.

Miguel wished the holes in his nose were smaller. He didn't want to smell it; it was stinky. Albert was telling his father that they'd been hanging out at the river this afternoon.

"Tell 'em what you said," Albert said with a grin.

Miguel giggled, but he was embarrassed, too. "I just said I didn't know your dad owned the Rio Grande."

"What! I don't," Mr. King said, laughing.

"But your land . . . it goes all the way down into the water. And your dog jumped in it and Albert rode his horse in it."

"Well, we own the horse, Miguel, but the river owns itself. We're lucky to live on Rio Grande Boulevard. This was the old Prince house. One of the Princes was a United States governor of the territory. He lived up there in Santa Fe in the Palace of the Governors."

"I've been there!" Albert said proudly. "It's hundreds of years old."

"Now the Palace is a history museum where you find out some real interesting stuff about Mexico and the U.S., Miguel," Mr. King said, proudly. "I'll take you and Albert sometime."

"Miguel doesn't like history, Dad," Albert said, interrupting gently.

"Well, you'd like this kind of history, son. It talks right at you."

"Is Santa Fe on the Rio Grande, too?" Miguel asked. He was thinking of the river at the edge of the Kings' property. It was the one Dad had carried him across on his shoulders five years ago. The same river flowed past El Paso where Joey Jeter's dad guarded the border. And here it was several hundreds of miles north. Still the same one—in Albuquerque—where Mom had brought them two and a half years ago after the immigration officers had visited the apartment and scared her.

"No. Santa Fe's above the river. High up. Tell us about your family," Mr. King said, shooting a look at Albert, who was on his second helping already. Miguel was hardly eating anything. "Albert King! Sit up and pay attention. We're having dinner table conversation—something you never learned at your mother's."

Albert's pink face flamed. "I am paying attention, Pop!"

"Yes, you are. Good!" He winked at Miguel, who quickly stuffed in a big bite of food. "You have any brothers or sisters, Miguel?"

Miguel's mouth was full.

"He's got twin sisters, six years old, and a sister who's sick," Albert said.

"Sorry to hear that, son. I hope she gets better," Mr. King said. "Your folks are here, right?"

Miguel was thinking about María Contenta, who wouldn't eat if he wasn't home. Hearing Mr. King's question, he said, "My mother sews at the México Fantastico Flea Market and Bargain Bazaar. She's making pretty drapes and the king and queen bedspreads for people."

"I've heard of it. And what about your father? Where's he?"

Miguel swallowed a bite of meat he'd taken. It was painfully hard to hack out the words, "He's *away.*"

"What do you mean *away*? Where? Divorced like my mom and dad?" Bucky said, suddenly interested in the talk, but the table went silent, everybody looking at Miguel.

Albert glared at his brother.

"Looks like your buddy's lost his appetite," Bucky said.

"Sorry. I am a slow eater," Miguel said, sweat popping out on his forehead, a queasiness floating into his stomach. He hid the green jelly under his potato skin.

"You moved from El Paso a couple years ago, Albert says. Your English is good, son," said Mr. King, clearing his throat.

"I try, Mr. King, but I've got a Mexican accent and I make too many mistakes."

"You do not. You talk great," Albert said, surprising him. He had offered to call Miguel *Mike* so the other kids wouldn't know for sure he was from Mexico, but Miguel was too self-conscious to do that.

Suddenly a made-up answer to Mr. King's question about where Dad was popped into Miguel's head. Heart pounding, he said proudly, "My dad's a teacher. He teaches in El Paso. Teaches third grade. Likes history and the sports. Basketball's his best. He played on a team once. He's remarried. They got a little kid."

Albert looked really surprised at that.

Bucky said, "Just what I thought. Left your mom with all the kids and no money." He sounded suspicious and a little angry. Miguel's eyes opened wide, shocked at Bucky's words.

"Shut up, Bucky, you horse's ass! You got no manners or feelings?" Mr. King said, only a bit more gently than Bucky had said his words.

Albert shot a dirty look at Bucky and said to Miguel, "Tell Dad what your mother bought you."

Miguel was sensing hard feelings in this family. He suddenly worried that Mr. King would guess that Miguel's father didn't speak English well enough to be a teacher and would catch him in a lie.

"Miguel, tell 'em what your mom got you," Albert said again.

"Oh! A bike, so I can get away from the kids who hate me."

Miguel looked down at his plate. The lamb grease had coagulated. It looked like hard white fat that sticks to a lard can. He made three more bites disappear into his mouth.

The room was quiet, solemn as a church almost. He took a deep breath and finished off all the rest of the meal. Except for the jelly. Then he folded up his napkin like Mr. King's and placed it beside the plate.

He couldn't wait to go home. *I don't talk about Dad to nobody.*

That night Oprah Rivera cried out, "Miguel! Miguel! Come! Quick, Miguel! Hurry, hurry, hurry!" She was in the bedroom.

Mom had left for the grocery store as soon as Miguel came home after dinner. He was in charge. Rosa's employer had given them the tiny apartment in the Mexican neighborhood when they ran away from El Paso. They had arrived in Albuquerque expecting to find Crístobal Rivera waiting for them at Señor Fantastico's. Their father seemed to have disappeared, leaving no trace.

When Crístobal never showed up, Señor Fantastico felt terrible.

"Take this apartment, Rosa, for you and your children," the old Mexican man had said, with tears rolling down his cheeks. "No rent. I help you. Don't be *escared*," his mother's employer had promised.

"Miguel!" Oprah screamed from the bedroom.

"Coming! Coming!" He ran to the cot in the corner of the crowded room to see what was wrong. He found ten-year-old María Contenta writhing on the bed, her legs and arms shivering and twitching.

"What's the matter? What's the matter!" Oprah said, her eyes full of fear, clinging to Miguel's arm.

"No, nothing. Don't worry, Oprah! She's having a seizure." Miguel knelt beside María and tilted her head back, to be sure she could breathe. Then he put her arm nearest him under her side and slid it under her hips. He lay the other arm across her chest and crossed her leg farthest from him over the near one at the ankle.

"This is the recovery position Dr. Leroy showed us," he told Oprah, who was crying for her poor sister. "You do it real, real gentle," he added.

Carla was now awake and out of bed, too, pushing in next to her twin sister to see.

Miguel grasped María's soft nightgown at the hip and supported her head while pulling her toward him. She rested against his knees. He kept her from rolling on her face. In a little while she was breathing deeply, and then her soft brown eyes opened.

"She doesn't know what happen," Miguel said in a low voice.

"That's kind of good. Don't you think so, Miguel?" Carla whispered.

"Yeah, we don't want her to know how bad a seizure looks, poor thing!" Oprah said, Miguel nodding in agreement.

"Papa?" María said. "Papa . . ." She always asked for Crístobal. They could never say he's here.

She sat up, looked around and smiled. Miguel and the twins gave her kisses and pats and brought her grape juice with ice chips to drink. They had to smash the ice cubes with a hammer to make the chips because that was her favorite.

2

July *Fortaleza*

It was so hot in Albuquerque, Miguel had stripped down to his undershorts. The family was in the crowded bedroom, the girls already asleep. Mom and he were wide awake, hoping for a breeze through a narrow window that overlooked the busy street below.

"I remember Dad carrying me on his shoulders over the Rio Grande. I was five, Mom," he said.

"What a memory you got!" she said. Brushing her long black hair, she sat cross-legged on her air mattress in the tiny room. They had the TV low. She wouldn't miss Carla Aragón on Channel 4 news.

"Know why I remember? Because when Albert and I go down to the Rio Grande the sound brings the memory back," he said.

"What sound?" she said, frowning. She was twisting her hair into a cool braid.

"*Swisha. Swisha.* When we crossed the river from Mexico— remember? We couldn't talk, we couldn't say anything. And that sound sticks in my memory. It was nice, Mama."

"Like music?"

"Uh huh."

"The Rio Grande," she said dreamily. "We see it in Mexico. Then we see it from the bridge in El Paso. And now, here it flow past Albuquerque, New Mexico. It want to be with us, no?"

He didn't tell her, but the river called to him.

In its slow, swirling brown waters he saw the face he used to see in the steamed-up bathroom mirror. *"What happened to my dad?"* he begged the face to answer every time. *"Where's Dad? Where is he?"*

The water-face refused to speak to him now. He didn't know why. He dreamed of sailing down the Rio Grande to Mexico and finding Dad. He dreamed of riding Mr. King's most powerful horse there. He was sure somehow that Dad was in Mexico and needed Miguel to rescue him.

Tonight he finally felt the courage to ask his mother what she thought. His voice was strong, insisting. "Mom! *What* happened to Dad?"

Only a month after they had arrived in Albuquerque, she had stopped talking about Crístobal Rivera. She said at the time in her loudest voice, "Look! I no talk about him no more. I can no think about him no more. I have to be strong as both the woman and the man. Strong as two people. At the same time. Is *all* my responsibility now. Everything. No one else's."

When they never heard even one word from him or about him, Miguel guessed his mother thought that he was dead. But tonight he wanted to know her thoughts.

"I do not know what thing happened to him!" she said angrily, throwing her head back. And then, a moment later, shaking her head sorrowfully, saying, "No idea." Then in a trembly voice she added, "Not one!"

"I think of him all the time, Mom."

The mystery of Crístobal Rivera's disappearance swirled constantly around him the way the river teased and tossed bugs, rodents, and birds that fell into it and drowned. "You must have a guess, Mom."

"Is true, but I no say guess-words out loud. I am afraid. My heart is a land of tragedies. But God leave you, my beautiful girls, and the sewing machine with me. All that give me hope and thanks. *Muchas gracias!*" Her dark eyes filled with tears, and now he knew how sad it made her that Crístobal had disappeared.

"*Mi madre* teach me *fortaleza*. You know what that is, Miguel? *Fortaleza?*" she asked dramatically, her eyes flashing like an actress's in a movie.

Nodding, he said, "*Fortaleza.* Fortitude." He took a deep, deep breath. Did he know it? She said it all the time.

She smiled. "I have taught you something then—the persistence. *Los Méxicanos* have to have it. The great César Chávez, hero to the migrant workers, said, "Yes, you can!" Little tiny words, full of power. *Yes, you can!* To anything. Even without *mi esposo Crístobal,* your *padre,* I say, "Now our lives, like the flowers, is blooming. Like the red ones in Zacatecas. My son is a tree growing the strong branches and the deep roots. Just like your father, except that *you* going to be a happy man. Not like my *pobre Crístobal.* This I promise you, Miguel."

Miguel hated it when she talked like that. He didn't believe it.

Miguel and Albert built a raft out of timber and sheets of plastic in the middle of July. They wanted to sail the Rio Grande. But the water was so shallow, the raft stuck in the mud.

They also played baseball on a Little League Team and came in second place. They could have won if they had not had to go to summer school for six weeks. They had both failed fifth grade math. Miguel had also failed social science.

At the time of his report card, his mother, shaking her head, said, "Even though you so smart, Miguel, you fail." Her expression wasn't even angry, but bewildered, her voice soft for a change. "Is a good thing maybe. It make you humble. The boys get big ideas about their power. They show the world their muscles and their armpits."

"Come on, Mom!" he had protested.

"Armpits, yes! They say power. Boys, they show off to everybody. Looka me! Looka me! Then they forget their spiritual parts and the higher truth. Then they no try to be better human beings and give love and kindness. Maybe is good you fail something now."

Miguel had squirmed and remembered Tortugas School and Mr. Springley. Back then he had worked to get good grades and sometimes succeeded.

He also remembered the auto parts yard Dad guarded at night, and he remembered the horrible men running out the gate after they had beaten him. He remembered the awful morning his father had left home to escape the smugglers—the beginning of the end for them in El Paso.

Rosa turned down her bed and told Miguel to hurry up and get into his. "Lights off now. I need good sleep because pretty soon I learn to ski. One day very, very soon the Riveras be snow-deep in Santa Fe."

"Aw, Mom!" he said, shaking his head in irritation.

"You never believe we going to get there because we still poor. But . . ." She leaned over to kiss his cheek.

"But what, Mom?" he whined, dropping his head on his pillow with a sigh.

"I know things you do not know. Señor Fantastico has a big idea. I tell you very soon what it is." She kissed him good night and added, "Don't worry so much!"

"Even in Santa Fe there will be guys who hate wetbacks."

She slapped her hands together and pushed them against his chest. "Don't use that word ever again. You be strong, Miguel!"

"I am strong!" he yelled back, completely doubting it for that moment. He felt like a pussycat, not like a strong boy about to turn eleven. "*They* do. *They* use it!" he said angrily, rolling over and closing his eyes.

Folding her nightgown carefully under her knees, Rosa knelt down beside her bed and prayed in whispers. "Let no mean kids be in Santa Fe! Please, dear *Padre Dio!* And thank you for us soon moving from the river. I don't want that boy do something crazy. Please!"

Rosa already knew that they would be moving before sixth grade started for Miguel. She was afraid to say it aloud until the plans were firm. Her heart ached for Miguel, her sweet boy, looking more like Crístobal every day. So handsome! A good boy! Such a good boy! She was trying very hard to keep any more disappointments from him.

Part Three

MIGUEL IN SANTA FE ENCOUNTERING ENEMIES AGAIN

1

Here He Is, Ready or Not

Miguel Rivera's heart was in his mouth. He had awakened in Santa Fe, New Mexico, remembering what Bucky King, Albert's brother, had told him. "You'll see stuck-up guys in Santa Fe, their noses in the air, Miguel. Santa Fe guys! The worst snobs in New Mexico."

Miguel hoped he was exaggerating. It had been only four weeks since Rosa Rivera had hinted this move would happen. And *bing bang boom* here he was! He'd already enrolled in a middle school he knew was going to be way tougher for him to fit in than the little school in Albuquerque. He'd be a hundred before he found a buddy like Albert King again.

In Santa Fe, Señor Fantastico opened a México Fantastico Bargain Store (without the flea market because a big one was already here). It was near the restaurants and the farmer's market. He made Rosa Rivera the buyer of fabrics *and* the seamstress *and* the designer of draperies. He loved her beautiful work, and her salary doubled.

A day after the twins' sixth birthday, August 15, Rosa moved Miguel and the three girls into beautiful Santa Fe. She chose a used trailer that ACCION—a charity for people struggling to be self-sufficient—was helping her purchase with a loan.

"I feel like a real American with a mortgage," she said, laughing when they set up their new home. Afterwards she led Miguel to the last room in the mobile home, all the way in the back. Her eyes were shiny as she opened the door with a grand sweep.

"*This* is your room," she said tenderly. "When you close the door, no person will open it. It is private. It is yours, *hijito*. All yours."

"I don't have to sleep with the girls?" he said, his eyes wide.

"No! Your sisters have their own room," she said proudly.

"Wow! Wow! WOW, Mom!" he shouted, jumping up and touching the ceiling of his room.

They painted it a reverberating Mexican blue. He hung up baseball players' pictures. She made him a red, yellow, and tan quilt with bold blue zigzags. There were blue pillow shams on the bed and a pine desk in the corner. He rubbed it with Johnson Paste Wax until Rosa and the girls could see a drop of water standing on top and not sinking into the wood. The red curtains had blue fringes.

"But no TV!" he complained, wrinkling his nose. "No computer? No telephone?"

Rosa yelled, "You buy that *junque* with your own money!" She stomped out of the room until he caught her and thanked her.

"The room looks just like one I saw for the President on TV."

"What president?" she said, suspiciously.

"The President of Santa Fe!" he said.

"Who?" she said, knitting her dark eyebrows together.

"Me!" he said with a big grin.

"Oh! You! You crazy boy! You so bad!" she said, kissing his cheek without bending over. He was suddenly almost as tall as she was.

2

Indian Leg Wrestling in
Official Santa Fe

In Santa Fe, the capital of New Mexico, new people moved into town in the fall. They started college or new jobs or sometimes they were transferred to work in Santa Fe. On the third Saturday of a golden September, a new government-issue desk and a modern swivel chair were placed in the offices of the United States Immigration and Naturalization Service. The offices overlooked Lincoln Avenue. That street led to the Plaza and the big Palace of the Governors at the corner.

The Palace and town plaza were built in 1610 to house the Spanish governor, and the explorers and settlers. Seventy years later the Pueblo Indians cut off their water supply and took over the Palace in a revolt, until the Spanish won it back. Now descendants of those Indians sat under the roof of the historic building's portal selling their jewelry and pottery.

In his new office in the Immigration and Naturalization Service, a trim man, sporting a black, nipped mustache, invited his red-headed, muscular son inside. They were eating chicken carnitas sold by a vendor next to the Palace of the Governors.

"Joey, bring those file boxes under the window so I can unload them into my desk. Everything ready for Monday!" Second Lieutenant Richard Cortés spoke like a general and did not waste time.

"Right away!" his son said. He didn't waste it either.

Lieutenant Cortés poked a toothpick in between his left molars to release a stringy piece of meat. (His dental hygienist had advised him to use extreme caution in this operation so that he did not uproot a filling. This time, he didn't.)

He tossed the carnita wrapper into his coyote fur-wrapped wastebasket—a farewell gift from his unit in El Paso. Cortés was the primary investigator of "coyotes" from Mexico who smuggled workers into the United States. This was a cruel, expensive, and dangerous operation, with many desperately poor workers dying while crossing the boiling hot desert. Lieutenant Cortés collected information to prosecute the smugglers.

His eleven-year-old son bent over to lift up the stack of three bulging cartons at one time. "Where?" he said, breaking into a sweat, stumbling from the weight.

"Right here! You didn't hear me the first time?"

"Yes, I did. Just being sure, sir." Joey Jeter Cortés lowered the load of cartons next to the desk. His heart pounded. "Wow!"

His father had opened the file to receive official papers. They spent an hour arranging the files of people who had been smuggled in crowded, miserable vehicles across various American borders. Although there were thousands of these people, Lieutenant Cortés was interested in illegal immigrants who had come in through Arizona. Some of them resided in New Mexico, but many had disappeared altogether.

When they finished the work, Joey said, "Hey, Dad! Want to wrestle?"

They whipped off their jackets, flung them on the desk, and stretched out on the hard floor next to each other. "My father never taught me any sport," Lieutenant Cortés said. "Indian leg wrestling lets your enemy know your strength without hurting him very much. Ready?"

By the time they were both caught in the other's hold, Lieutenant Cortés was huffing and puffing. "The heart or the lungs," he said mournfully. "This high altitude is winding me."

"Maybe it's your age, Dad, 'cause *this* is my favorite sport," Joey

Jeter Cortés said, slamming his father's leg down on the mat—or floor actually—and holding it there.

It was the first time that Lieutenant Richard Cortés hadn't pinned his son first. "Whew!" he said, surprised at how mad it made him. "Time you did this with people your own age, I think," he grumbled.

"But I like wrestling you!" Joey Jeter hooked his leg and pinned him again. "That's two! I'm almost ahead," he said. "You got me beat by only twenty to two now."

"Humpffhh!" his father said, lacking anything more important to say. "That's a lot."

"I'm gonna do it, Pop! Can't wait!" Joey Jeter crowed, knowing his dad was miffed and enjoying it. Every time they did anything, his dad had to say, "My father never taught me sports." *Boring! Listening to that whiny stuff over and over.*

Lieutenant Cortés, latching on to his desk chair, pulled himself up.

Snapping his fingers, Joey saluted and said, "I'm going for another carnita, Dad. Pick me up at the Plaza when you're ready to go home, okay? Guys at school registration yesterday said they hang out there."

"Which guys?"

"Like back home. *No* wetbacks, wetbacks, wetbacks!" he said with a big grin.

The word *wetbacks* seemed to slide down the walls like water leaking through the roof.

"Wetbacksss, sweatbacks, sweatbacksss," Joey Jeter repeated, mesmerized by the sounds.

Lieutenant Cortés frowned and spoke sternly. "What're you doing?"

Joey Jeter blushed. "Nothing."

"I am assigned an important duty here in the capital city. So, as *my* son, be careful of who you associate with. We don't want any trouble reflecting on my parental training of you. Understand?"

Still daydreaming a little, Joey Jeter wondered if the way his dad had said *my* son meant the MY was as important as the SON, or even more important.

"Joey!" his father barked.

Joey snapped to and stood erect. "I do and I will continue to understand and obey." He reeled off the line like a telephone recording reels off numbers.

His father beamed. "That's the answer, mister! Good! Five o'clock then. Northwest corner of the Plaza."

"Righto!"

That same Saturday afternoon Albert King, in a spiky haircut, stood on the stepping stone to Miguel's mobile home. He had come from Albuquerque, a backpack with pajamas in it on his shoulders. Before driving off in his sporty car, Albert's father, Mr. King, tooted his horn and waved at the Riveras.

Miguel lifted his arm and waved back at Mr. King. "Thanks for bringing Albert to see us!" he shouted.

"You better not snore and keep me awake, buddy," Albert said with a big, happy grin on his face as he followed Miguel inside.

"How's it goin' back in Albuquerque?" Miguel said.

"Not so hot back in Albuquerque. How's it goin' here in the capital city?"

Miguel shook his head. "It stinks. But hey, you're here! We can look around. I haven't been to the Plaza yet, but I seen this dribbly thing they call the Santa Fe River. It's not like *our* river. They got a good place to skateboard here. We can buy carnitas on the street, Mom says."

"*I* want to see your school." Albert didn't say he'd already visited the Plaza a hundred times. His grandmother lived near the center of old Santa Fe in a retirement home, and family friends lived close by on Palace Avenue, too.

"Oh, no! We're not going to that school," Miguel muttered.

Rosa shouted, "Lunch is ready!" and served up corn tamales and guacamole with chips. Everybody was stuffed and fell asleep before midnight.

Sunday morning the boys woke up late and fixed their own breakfast. Rosa had taken the girls to church and left a note with bus money for them. They caught the noon bus to the Plaza, but got off before it arrived to play one-on-one with some little kids in a playground. Afterwards they jogged the mile to the Plaza.

"I'm on my own this year. The teacher has us working really hard on homework, and all the kids I like are in the other sixth grade," Albert said.

"That's too bad!" Miguel said, his eyes dark and his voice low. "It was better in fifth grade, wasn't it?"

"You're right," Albert said, worried that he shouldn't have brought the subject up, because Miguel looked grim suddenly. Miguel had been biting his nails on the bus and looking half-scared ever since he'd got there. When they were finally at the Plaza, Albert saw him stare at the long covered portal in front of the Palace of the Governors.

"That Palace looks like old buildings do in Mexico. Who are all the people sitting in front under the roof?" Miguel said in a small voice.

"Indian artists. They come from the pueblos here in New Mexico and some from the Navajo lands. Let's see what they're selling."

Miguel, keeping a safe little distance behind Albert, followed him as they crossed the grassy square under the leafy trees.

"Look at the things they make. A lot of people come here just to see the Indians and collect their jewelry and clay pots and rugs. People from all over the world buy from them."

"Are you sure?"

"Why? It's true, though it wasn't always. Pop says it was pretty tough for the Indians when he was a boy." Albert looked at Miguel and wondered about the question he had asked.

Miguel was shocked to learn that the Indians here were admired. How different from Mexico! He knew that the Indians there were often looked down upon and nobody wanted to be them.

At one-thirty they met Albert's father at La Fonda Hotel on the southeast side of the grassy Plaza. He bought them hamburgers in the sunny courtyard of the hotel restaurant, and later ice cream. "What say we go over to see the Palace of the Governors museum now? Do we have time?" he said.

Albert shook his head. "Let's do it next time, Pop. We gotta go. I have a ton of homework. Sorry, Miguel!"

"Come back soon, Albert, okay? Will you?" Miguel said, his heart starting to pound knowing his friend had to leave.

Mr. King said, "We'll be back, son. Next time we'll see the museum in the Palace. I can show you Governor Prince's sitting room. Do you remember our talking about that, Miguel?"

"I sure do!"

When Albert left the Plaza for Albuquerque in his dad's old maroon Lancia sportscar, Miguel stared after them, emptiness gnawing at his stomach. Wearing his yellow *panuelo,* or bandana, around his head, he sneaked looks at the guys on the Plaza. They were playing Hacky Sack near the Civil War Monument. A boy in an orange shirt skateboarded around the pavement separating the green and leafy Plaza from the street and its cars. The sunshine was melting through the trees and warming the ornate green benches. People reading tourist maps stopped in front of the Palace of the Governors and then went inside it.

Those who didn't go inside stopped and looked at the silver and turquoise jewelry and the clay pots being sold by the Indian vendors in front of the Palace. Miguel watched them for a long time.

He wiped his sweaty face with a corner of the *panuelo.* A booming radio somewhere was playing jazz saxophone music. He listened, trying to figure why people in America loved jazz so much.

His mother had admonished him to be wary of the kids who hung out in the Plaza. "They may not be nice or friendly," she had said. Sitting on the bench now, he felt the cold loneliness of being new to Santa Fe and the Ortiz Middle School. Albert's brother, Bucky, was right. Kids from Santa Fe acted tough and smart just because they lived here in the capital. Sooner or later Miguel knew he was going to be picked on and even kicked around. Last night, sizing up Albert, who was taller and stronger than he was, Miguel felt he'd better work out. He needed to get some weights, a bench, and bigger muscles fast.

He squinched his eyes, catching thoughts of Dad. *If he doesn't come home, how am I going to get to be a man?* His throat tightened. He bit his bottom lip and shut his eyes against everything he could see, wishing his worries would disappear forever and, sadly then, wishing that he, himself, could fade away, too.

Near the monument, a bear-shaped boy played Hacky Sack. He was stocky and wore a striped black-and-white tee shirt over denim shorts. Although he was just thirteen, his legs and arms were hairy. A skinny kid wearing a similar striped shirt teased him, saying, "You smooth those hairs down like a girl and look at 'em in the mirror, don't you?"

"I do not!" the Bear said, laughing.

"Oh, yes you do!"

"Get out of here, Wrench! You're jealous 'cause your spindle-shanks are bare-naked," the Bear said.

"No, they're not," the kid retorted.

"Oh, okay, just invisible," the Bear said. He was proud of the hair. It had appeared overnight and it almost did make him a man. He was looking for hair on his chest, too. But now he was bored and kept muttering, "Come on! Let's go do somethin' else."

His friend didn't pay any attention until the Bear came up with an idea. He pointed out Miguel sitting on the bench with his eyes squeezed shut. "Hey, see that kid sleepin' over there. He's probably drunk."

"That *mojado*? He can't afford a drink," the skinny boy said.

"We can beat him up. He's in my English class at Ortiz and fakes smart. Comes from the Juárez slums, I bet. He's wearing that jerky yellow *panuelo*," the Bear said.

"What's his name? José Wetback?" the boy said, laughing. He had a fiery rash on his cheek from allergies and he wasn't supposed to scratch it, but his hand was always up there. His hands were strong, too, and did damage to his face. He could twist your arm into a pretzel. That's why guys called him the Wrench.

A new boy who they'd seen yesterday hanging around the park came up. He was a big, freckled redhead in a Yankees cap. He told them, "We used to beat on those guys in El Paso. It was cool." He pointed to Miguel.

"I didn't know anybody but Mexi-punks live in El Paso," the Bear said, laughing again.

"Proves you don't know anything. I lived there," the new guy said, blue eyes glaring.

"What's your name?" a tall, blond skateboarder said, wiping the sweat off his face with the tail of his orange shirt. He had joined them, and it seemed to relieve the tension.

"Joe Cortés. I'm starting Ortiz tomorrow. Any of you go there?"

"All of us."

"Not me! I'm at Prep," the skateboarder said.

"Watch it, Preppy. We'll get you," the Bear said with a cracky laugh.

The skateboarder said, "Let's get that kid over there instead. But first I'm heading to the hotel to hit the restroom. Meet you back here." He took off toward La Fonda Hotel.

When he failed to return, the Bear said, "I knew he wouldn't come back. If Jonathan gets in trouble, his dad will string him up and let the ravens peck his eyes out. So come on! Let's get that kid. It's up to the three of us to defend our park and keep the wetbacks out!"

3

A Fight

Miguel had dozed off when he felt the bench tilt back suddenly and hit the ground with a bang. His eyes flew open and he was looking at the Wrench and the red-haired kid. Miguel squinted at the redhead's face. It was familiar.

"Hey! What d'you want? I ain't bothering you!" he yelled, trying to regain his balance and sliding off into the grass instead.

"We're Sanitation. Cleaning up the Plaza. Gotta go, you're trash," the Bear said, bumping hard into Miguel's crumpled legs.

The Wrench leaned down and jammed a finger into Miguel's chest.

"Oww!" Miguel, caught by surprise, managed to squirm away and jump up. "Leave me alone!"

People walking through the Plaza veered off to avoid the gang of boys. The three surrounded Miguel, menacing him.

He put up his hands. "Okay, okay. I'm out of here. To meet a friend of Governor King."

The boys jeered.

"He's not the governor now! That was years ago," the Bear said, bumping him hard again. It was humiliating.

Breathing hard, Miguel turned and walked toward the street in front of the Palace of the Governors with as much dignity as he could muster. It wasn't a whole lot. When he peered back, the gang was watching him. He ran into the street and dodged a slow-moving gray pickup going west and a white convertible heading east.

He dashed under the covered portal of the museum and bumped into a girl looking at the Indians' wares.

"Hey, boy, can you please be careful?" the girl said. Her voice sounded brave, he thought.

But Miguel didn't answer. He couldn't. He saw the gang coming after him. He ran around the corner to Washington Street wondering where to hide. He was too new to the town. Passing the one-story buildings on the left, he saw a ramp to an underground garage in a taller office building. He zoomed down the ramp. *They will think I disappeared into thin air. Ee-wow!*

The dim garage had only six or seven cars in it. It was Sunday: open and free to the public. His heart sank when he realized there were no guards. As he ran toward the exit far across the big garage, he heard shouts and spun around. Crouching like wild animals prowling, the three boys came at him.

He dodged behind a green car and ducked down, ready to roll underneath. Two of them piled on top of him. The Wrench grabbed his arm and twisted it as far as it would go. Miguel screamed. The Bear shoved his open palm against Miguel's nose.

"Owww!" Miguel cried, tears popping. "Let go! Let go of me!"

"*Mojado!* Go back where ya came from!" said the Bear.

"Okay! Let me go! Please!"

The redhead yanked off Miguel's *panuelo* and ground it under his shoe. "I *know* you!" he said with the voice of triumph.

Miguel stared back in recognition, too.

"You're Miguel uh . . . ?" the boy said. "I got it! Guys! Meet Miguel from hell."

"And I know **YOU! Joey Jeter Cortés!**—the **Biggest Poop in Texas!**"

Joey Jeter Cortés was stunned.

Miguel managed to yank his aching arm away from the Wrench and shoved him against a car. His head smacked the glass, and the Wrench yelled, "Owww!"

The other boys tried to pound Miguel's back, but he took off running, nearly colliding with two women parkers. They gasped when he flew past with blood on his face.

"I'm calling the police!" one of the women announced in a furious voice.

The pursuers were stopped for a moment.

Miguel reached the top of the exit ramp on Lincoln Avenue and ran back toward the Plaza. He dodged passersby on the tree-lined street and came to the Palace of the Governors. It spanned the whole block.

Albert's Dad said the Palace is public. Does it mean I can go in?

Wiping blood off his face with his shirtsleeve, he raced, panting, past the Indian artists selling in the cool shadows under the roof.

The doors are open!

He flew inside the Palace of the Governors.

An Hispanic man, as tall and thin as Miguel's father, stood in the vestibule. His dark eyes smiled a welcome.

"I want to see the museum, *sir*, please?" Miguel said.

"Sorry, my boy," the guard said regretfully when he realized Miguel was alone. "Children under sixteen are not allowed inside the museum without an adult."

4

Mystery Words

"Please! I'm waiting for somebody, mister," Miguel gasped.

The guard tilted his head.

"For my dad!" That sounded important.

The man nodded and went down the slanting floor to the admission counter inside the museum. "Okay," he said over his shoulder. "You can wait here. That's fine."

Miguel leaned against a thick adobe wall supporting the dark beamed ceiling. On either side of the hallway a doorway opened on an exhibit, but no one entered the museum that way. He squinted, peering beyond the Palace doors to the street to see if he'd been followed.

He did not have to look hard because he heard shouting.

"Hey, Miguel-Mudface! Get out here!" Across from the Palace, the boys stood on the curb, arms against their chests. Miguel pressed himself to the ancient fortress wall for protection. He slid along the wall to the doorway on the left. A room was on display there. Slender posts supporting a railing across the door frame, halfway up, kept visitors on the outside of the room. A sign said: "Office of the Mexican Governor."

Mexican governor? Are they loco? This is New Mexico. He was so baffled he wanted to yell at somebody. Sweat dribbled down his face. Out of the corner of his squinting eyes, he spotted the Bear across the street, his face red, mouth wide open.

They're not going to give up! At least they can't come inside the

Palace of the Governors.

He whipped his head around to check for the guard. Not in sight. Seeing no one entering the museum, and no one leaving, Miguel grabbed the rail and leaped over it and into the Mexican Governor's office. He hunkered down on the hard mud floor, flattening his hot back against the cool adobe wall. Tears stung his eyes. He squeezed them shut. The tears sneaked down his cheek anyway. He covered his face with a dirty hand and cried. *Stupid! Stupid! Qué pasa? I'm a baby again?*

The truth of his predicament washed over him. All his joy was gone. He was alone! Despised.

Hopeless in an old room smelling of dust and people gone a long time ago. A woolen brown-and-white checked rug lay on the floor. A small wooden table and old straight chairs furnished the room. Light came through a window on to the Palace portal and street. Nothing looked comfortable and everything was plain. Halfway up, the walls were red, then they were white. An old trunk resting on a stand against a wall reminded him of something. But he couldn't remember what. A T-shaped wooden candelabra had stubby candles on it and hung from the ceiling. A rope to lower it was attached to the wall.

He stared at the trunk decorated with paintings of flowers and ten men in black hats and suits, sitting in a canoe. His mother had told him about her family trunk. It had been left behind in Mexico. "We carried nothing we love across the river that night we come across the border, *mi 'jito*, except for you! In that precious old trunk, I had saved *Mama's* picture and her beautiful lace wedding veil, the same one I wore. A pretty book for *niños* was in the trunk, too. Papa gave it to me on the day when you were born."

Would his mother feel a little bit better if she could come to the Palace and see this trunk? The sign said it came from Mexico. Maybe it was a little like the one she gave up. He trembled. Mama depended on him now. As a man. She needed him. He was the family's protection. He had to be smarter than these guys. He couldn't let them get him.

After a while his mind drifted to the important man who had worked in this office long ago. *What was he like, the governor?* Instead of a stranger, he pictured his long lost dad in an old soldier's uniform sitting at the table in the shadowy room. *What would I say if my dad were the governor? Lock 'em up, Governor Rivera! Put them in the dungeon under the Palace and feed 'em tortillas and water.* At that, he grinned and then fell serious again. *I have to get out of here somehow, Papa, without those guys knowing it!* He sighed deeply and slapped at his eyes. He was teary again.

A fireplace was tucked in a corner. In his mind he set fire to the wood stacked in it to keep Papa warm and to give him light. *"Dad! I hate my life. I liked it when I had you and Mr. Springley. Now it's nothing. You promised you'd be with me! Why'd you forget!"*

Longing for his father burned inside him. Finally he murmured to the dead air, "If you're not coming back, can't you make it stop hurting!"

"Rivera's a coward! *Pendejo-mojado!*" he heard from the street.

I am not a coward! How can I sneak out of here into the main part of the museum and escape?

No door connected this room to the inside of the Palace. He could only go out the way he had come in. Worn with fear, he pulled himself up to stand and relieve his aching, knotted legs. How long before the guard discovered him? He'd be yanked into the street! He was in terrible, terrible trouble.

The shouting stopped. He waited, counting seconds. *One, two . . . fifty, fifty-one . . .* Nothing else. Suddenly, something stirred the stale air. Light flickered. Over the racket of his pounding heart, Miguel heard a voice faint with effort. *Don't give up, muchacho! Your padre does not forget what he promised.*

Miguel shivered. The air in the silent room trembled, too. He looked at the table. Nobody there.

I'm going crazy. I'm awake but that was a dream. A mistake. I'm a mistake. Miguel Rivera's mind said that, but his heart ignored his interpretation of everything as hopeless. His heart throbbed with *does not forget, does not forget, does not forget!* No matter what, his spirit was created stronger than the cruelty of mean boys. It added to its measured beat, *and will come back! Does not forget. And will come back! Does not and will* . . .

And then a real voice spoke to him. He spun around, expecting the guard to loom in the doorway.

5

Samson

A big blond teenager was leaning over the rail. "Hey! Hey, kid! What's the matter? What're you doing here? You'll get into trouble. You the kid they're yelling for in the street?" he whispered.

Miguel couldn't reply or stop crying. He nodded. "You know them?"

"Just two of their rotten brothers," the teenager said. "I told 'em to shut up. They were bugging everybody. Finally somebody came up and made them stop."

Miguel was filled with doubt. Had they sent this kid to get him?

"Nobody's looking right now," the teenager said, after checking the vestibule. "The guard's not here. Get out of there quick! Hurry!"

Miguel slipped over the rail and stood up. "How'd you know I was in here?"

"I guessed. I figured you were too young to get into the museum. You're the real Miguel Rivera, aren't you?"

"Yes!"

"Well, Albert King told me to look out for you."

"What! Albert came to see me last night."

"I know. See, my dad and Albert's are old buddies. Mr. King came to our house last night after he dropped Albert at yours, for dinner and to spend the night."

Miguel didn't know what to say. They stood in front of a framed poster with the words "Life in New Mexico, 1821–1846: The Mexican Period."

As several people passed behind them on their way out of the Palace, the boys pretended to study the poster. Then, concentrating, Miguel read the word *"Mexico."*

"Mexico?" he suddenly burst out. He had to know. "Hey! Do you know why it's saying Mexico when this is New Mexico?"

"Sure. It's the Mexican Period in Santa Fe."

"What's that?"

"The time when Mexico won its independence from Spain, remember? The Mexicans got tired of being conquered and took their country back from Spain. And they added New Mexico to their northern border for good measure. You didn't know that?" the boy said.

"I didn't know that."

"The Mexican Period didn't last long, but it must have been a lot of fun. Fiestas and fancy horse races and pretty women and dances!"

"Yeah!" Miguel said, as if those things were important to him, too.

"I wish I'd lived here then. Santa Fe had to be terrific when the Mexicans governed it." The kid grinned. "My great great great great-grandfather was here from Chihuahua, Mexico. A wild ladies man! Ran a dance hall."

"Didn't they try to throw him out?"

"Why? They loved him. He was important."

Miguel was amazed by what he'd heard. He went on reading the framed information: *The territory of New Mexico was expected to protect the newly free nation of Mexico from foreigners and hostile Indians. The times were peaceful and prosperous.*

"My name's Samson Anderson," the kid said in his low-pitched voice. He had thick blond hair clipped tightly to his head. His smile was big and his face, ruddy, as though he lived outdoors. His gray eyes shone. There was a fresh pink scar running from his nose halfway across his cheek. Like Albert's brother, Bucky King, Samson Anderson's features were neat and his mouth small. He wasn't tall but he looked strong. Miguel noticed his old jeans and a forest green tee shirt over a white collared shirt he wore. He smelled like peanuts. "Pretty hard to live up to Samson, right?"

"Pardon?" Miguel said.

"My name, Samson. My folks were nuts when they named ME that." He laughed. "Just call me Sam. I used to live in Santa Fe, but they've moved me to a private school because I couldn't get along here. I kept gettin' into trouble at Capitol High. Either I talked too much or I was too smart. Ha! Ha! This new school's in Okla-boring-homa. All I want to do is come back home to Santa Fe. They let me come for my birthday. Want some gum, Miguel?" he said, extending a red package.

Miguel took the gum gratefully; it was cinnamon. There was a taste like bullets in his mouth.

"You know his dad, but do you know Albert?" he said, finding it hard to believe this guy hadn't been sent into the museum by the mean boys to get him. It could have been a trick.

"Sure. All my life. I haven't hung out with him because he's younger and lives down there in Albuquerque."

"I showed him the Plaza today!" Miguel said.

"He's seen the Plaza before. His grandma lives here. Anyway, Mr. King brought pictures last night of you and Albert playing baseball. When I heard those kids shouting your name on the Plaza and heckling you, I wanted to find you. You look like they got at you some way."

Miguel bit his lip and didn't answer.

"Well, Miguel, not everybody in Santa Fe is mean. You got a friend now, even though I'm not here all the time."

Miguel had to smile then. *And I'm not dead yet.*

"Want to explore the Palace with me?" Samson Anderson asked. "I like to check out new exhibits."

"I gotta keep an eye on those guys."

"You can. From inside. I'll show you how."

6

Treasures

The Great Seal of New Mexico made of silver spoons, knives, and nails was shining on the wall. Sam Anderson took out the money to pay his admission. Miguel reached for his money, too.

"Oh, good! Your father did come!" the guard said, joking with them.

Miguel blushed and ducked his head. He'd explain later to Sam why the man had said that.

The gray-haired admissions clerk smiled. "Hi! New Mexico residents pay just a dollar on Sundays, but kids like you are always free," she said to Miguel. "We want you to come here. Kids are history happening!"

Sam gave Miguel a friendly nudge. He paid a dollar and they passed into a gallery with murals of mountains and trees. A huge wooden cart hauled on the rough trails long ago took up the gallery's space.

"You could hear these carts groanin' for three miles, they say. They traveled the Royal Road from Mexico to Santa Fe."

"I know that noise, Sam! Tía Yolanda Ana's grandfather had one. Mules pulled it up the hills behind the house. It was so loud it made my teeth hurt. No, feel funny. What's the word? Shiver?"

"Not shiver!" Sam laughed.

"Tingle! My teeth tingle. I forgot about his old cart," Miguel said.

They turned into the West Hallway. "Over here now!" Sam told

Miguel, his voice lowered to a dignified level. They glanced in the Governor Prince Room. "Look at that fancy parlor! The Princes lived here a long time ago," Sam said.

"Mr. King told me about Mr. Prince, the governor."

Sam pointed out a window in the hallway. "Look out! From this window—right here—see?"

"See what?" Miguel said, looking. "Ohhh! You can see the Plaza across the street. Cool! Cool."

"You can see when the monsters leave the Plaza, too."

"I'm callin' them the sore throats because of their mean voices."

"Right! Shame on 'em! They're just jerks."

When Sam said that, Miguel was glad and felt better. "They tried to . . . they beat me up, Sam."

"I guessed it. I thought that's what they were up to when I heard them yelling. Once the Bear's big brother threatened to steal the money I earned delivering newspapers," Sam said. "He scared me, but he didn't get it. My mouth saved me. I told him my dad was the chief of police and would slam him in jail. It wasn't true, but he believed me."

"Do you know my father or anything? I thought for a minute when I was inside the Mexican Governor's Office that he was with me," Miguel said in an aching voice.

Sam suddenly looked very serious, his eyes thoughtful and kind. Albert's dad had told him there was some mystery about Miguel's father. He spoke gently, saying, "I don't know him, no. But if I did, I'm sure I'd like him, Miguel."

He said that. But he did not tell Miguel that Albert had called him on a cell phone less than half an hour ago. The Kings were on their way home to Albuquerque. Albert had asked Sam to try to find Miguel in the Plaza. At the time Sam happened to be nearby in a coffee shop. Albert described what Miguel was wearing, saying Miguel was scared and really needed a friend.

"Is there a restroom? I'm all sweaty and dirty," he said, and Sam pointed the way. Miguel walked through the Palace's courtyard to the men's room. His face in the mirror shocked him. He used paper towels to clean up, tucked his shirt inside his pants and combed his hair. When he came out, he noticed the grassy garden and tall shade trees. It was beautiful and it felt wonderful to walk back into the big museum. He'd never been to a place like the Palace of the Governors before.

He rushed back to the hall window. While Miguel kept watch on the Plaza boys from the window, Sam was talking. "You can't stand here forever, man," he said. "Let's look at the exhibits. We'll come back and check on the guys later. They'll get bored and give up, or I can walk out of the Palace with you. Those chickens only gang up on one person at a time."

"I don't know," Miguel said, still staring out.

"Try it, okay?"

So Miguel moved away from the window with Sam still talking. He pointed to the buildings on the other side of the courtyard. "See the Palace Print Shop over there?"

Miguel nodded.

"They have a hand press. Pam, who runs it, teaches kids how to use it. It's the way newspapers were printed in the 1800s. Next time you come here, go in there."

They turned into a large gallery. "This show's called *Another Mexico*. They bring kids from around the state to see it."

"Why *Another* Mexico?" Miguel said, wrinkling his brow.

"Look at the map."

A beautiful gold-framed map hung on the wall. Miguel saw the word "Zacatecas" on the frame. Below it were hung pictures of the Mexican city, its mountains as high as Santa Fe's mountains.

Miguel shook his head in wonder. "I was born in Zacatecas, Sam. Why's the map *here*?"

"Wagon trains stopped in Zacatecas. The silver mines were there."

"I know. My dad's father worked in one," Miguel said.

"Merchants carried silver, salt, and other goods to sell on the Royal Road up to the capital here. Santa Fe—all of Texas, New Mexico, Arizona, Nevada, and California—were part of Mexico then, as you know."

"I told you I did NOT know that!" Miguel said, stopping still.

"What do you think New Mexico means anyway?" Sam said. "It's the *other* Mexico."

"I have to think about that," Miguel said, feeling better actually. He noticed the waxy smell of polish on the wide floorboards. It reminded him of the Johnson Wax he'd put on his own wooden desk at home. A nice smell, too. The floorboards groaned from age, making him think of the hundreds of people from the past who had walked on them.

Suddenly he remembered. "Hey! I got to check on the guys out there now." He left Sam and rushed back to the window. He looked but he couldn't find even one of his tormenters. *They've gone home? So I can, too!*

He turned, told Sam, and headed for the door. Sam was talking about what he had been thinking. "The kids in the Plaza were prejudiced against you, right? And some others were prejudiced against me in my high school here, too." Miguel comprehended the difference. "Those guys picking on you, Miguel, were showing off, trying to impress each other. They didn't even know you. They couldn't even SEE who you yourself really are. They figured you were *Méxicano*, that's all. Do people have to use their brains to know a person?" Sam asked.

"Well, I do," Miguel said, interested now.

"It takes brainwork, that's right. Some guys are so lazy."

Sam Anderson's ideas made sense. Miguel liked his deep voice, too, and was rethinking his figuring-out thoughts.

"Want to go to Starbucks and get a coffee?"

Miguel, surprised, recovered quickly. "Okay. I got some money."

"My cousin works there. She gets a discount. She'll give you one, too. I want you to meet her. Her name's Isabel Elise Atencio. Her mom's my mom's sister. Their family came to Santa Fe four hundred years ago. My dad came in 1983. Think of it! The Andersons came with the computers; the Chavezes with the conquistadors," he said, pretending to brandish a sword.

The other visitors in the museum were reading little descriptive signs beside the displays. He wanted to see what they said, too. "Can I meet her some other time, Sam?" he said carefully, not wanting to offend a person so nice to him.

"I fly back to Oklahoma tonight, Miguel. You have to meet her before I leave because you need somebody sixteen or over to bring you back here. We can't do the whole museum in one day, but it's important for you to come back."

"I can't come here. I help my mom after school."

"You have to come. Tell her. Isabel's smart. She'll know what to show you. She knows the history, because she learned it all to become the Fiesta Queen's Princess. You need to meet her. You don't understand, but you will. Come on!"

7

Isabel of Santa Fe

The cool air smelled woodsy and grassy after the old adobe building. His tormenters were gone so Miguel crossed the tree-filled Plaza like he owned it. Sam was explaining why they actually did.

"We own this Plaza, my dad says," Sam said, sliding some peanuts out of a bag and dropping them into his mouth. He offered the bag to Miguel, who refused politely. He was still chewing the gum.

"The part of Santa Fe that belongs to the city is ours and everybody else's. The Plaza was once the marketplace, and the wagon trains came here. They held horse races and bullfights right here."

"Bullfights! Eee-wow!"

"Blood and stink, no? The Spanish swapped goods to the Indians for their turquoise, leather moccasins, pottery, and stuff. Just like the Palace of the Governors belongs to the citizens; so does the Plaza. Nobody else owns it. It's not private; it's public. The people's." He munched peanuts at the same time he was talking.

"Huh!" Miguel said, remembering being dumped out of the park bench they were at the very moment passing. He put his hand out and stroked the cold wrought iron, noticing the words on the bottom of the back—*hecho en México*—made in Mexico.

On the other side of the Plaza and down a little was the coffee shop. Inside, Sam's cousin pointed them to comfortable brown leather armchairs in the corner. Sam's cousin Isabel brought them glasses of water right away and was introduced to Miguel. Her beautiful eyes were an indescribable gray—like lavender moonlight. She was so short—not even five feet tall—that Miguel was taller than she was.

While she was getting drinks and pastries for them, Sam confided to Miguel, "She's real small for her age, but one tough girl."

"She's pretty." Mysterious, too, he thought.

When Isabel brought back two cups of steaming hot chocolate, she said she could sit down with them for five minutes. "My boss has run to the corner, and Jimmy's taking orders so I get to have a rest. Waitressing is murder on your feet." She squeezed in next to Miguel, whose heart was pounding.

"Listen, Isabel. I brought Miguel here because he has to see the stuff on Mexico in the Palace. It's only a little matter of life and death."

"Really! Why?" she said, smiling at Miguel.

"Kids are dumping on him for being Mexican. And he's Albert King's best friend."

"Oh, Albert! Brother of Bucky, the handsome chef!"

"Right! Nobody's bothered to tell Miguel that Santa Fe was once a Mexican city. He's Mexican. It's important to know this. He's new in town and bullies are calling him a *mojado* and passing insults."

"That's abusive behavior! Oh, how terrible, Miguel!" Isabel said.

"He can't go to the museum alone, and you're sixteen and can take him."

"Seventeen. A woman."

"Will you take him, okay?"

"Sure! I want to be museum director one day. Or the governor and hand out money to our museums. Haven't decided which yet."

Miguel blinked. These Santa Fe kids were planners. She had a husky, soft voice that made him shiver with pleasure.

"Miguel!" she said. "Friday night we can do it. The museum's open at night and it's free. Okay? No matter how they mess you up in school—not the teachers, I mean, the doofy kids—you're going to get smart! It's the only thing that makes 'em respect you, Miguel."

At that moment, Joey Jeter Cortés and Lieutenant Cortés walked into the coffee shop and stood at the counter ordering. Miguel gasped and started to shake. He hadn't seen Joey's father, the INS Border Guard, since they were in Tortugas at the Fiesta of the Virgin of Guadalupe almost three years ago. The man hadn't changed.

"There he is. One of the guys who punched me," Miguel whispered to his new friends. "Joey Jeter Cortés. His father works for the Immigration and Naturalization Service."

Both Sam and Isabel spun around to see. "I'm going over to say hello. Just you wait here," Isabel said, jumping up. "Hello, gentlemen!" she said. "Can I help you?"

8

Smugglers

"Get up! Get out!" In urgent Spanish, furious with anger, the caller's fists pounded on the door of the shack. The padlock clicked open. The ratty door was kicked in.

"Why aren't you ready! We're loading up. *Vamonos!* Three minutes, *hombre!* We leave."

The man inside the cell moaned and rolled out. He was sore. He shook his hair and ran his fingers through its oily thickness and brushed off his pants and shirt. Over his head he pulled a stinking, mud-encrusted serape. It was cold. No moon. Very little sleep. He felt buzzy and confused.

After rubbing circulation into his bony feet, he put on rubber-soled sandals. Another furious shout at him, "Rivera! *Vamonos!*"

His shoes unhooked and flapping against his feet, Rivera ran into the dark. He quickly relieved himself and ran to the pick-up point. The smugglers always crashed the border just after midnight. *El capitano* snapped his whip, striking Rivera on the shoulder and cutting him again.

He headed for the pale yellow lights of the van being loaded in silence. There he helped push the men to be transported into the United States into the van. These workers did not speak Spanish; they had to be directed by force. Yesterday the boss had Rivera remove all the seats so they could get twenty-seven people standing inside this time—the most they had ever carried.

The desperate-for-work people squeezed in side by side. One of the younger workers to be transported tripped and fell. The whip caught him and at its sting he sobbed. Rivera hushed him. Dangerous. Unnecessary sound was forbidden. Punished.

He climbed into the van. He'd watch over them as they rumbled across the open Sonoran Desert to the border of Arizona. They did not use roads. Too risky! The Mexican patrols were becoming fiercer. The American Border Patrol's war against smugglers was hot and angry. They couldn't be bribed.

Rivera was handed a gallon jug of water to dispense among the thirsty. When they arrived at their secret destination with the smugglers north of the border in the U.S.A., he would do the talking. His Mexican Spanish was fine, and his second language worked, too. He could talk fast, and it was easy for Americans to understand.

This was his one hundred eightieth trip. Yesterday, the captain said that when he made his two hundredth trip he would be freed. He knew what that meant. They would shoot him dead in the trees half a mile away from camp. After his kidnapping and almost thirty-three months of slavery, he knew too much.

Tonight's smuggled workers came from across the Atlantic, from Afghanistan. They panted and sweated in the heat. One sang a monotonous song. When the door slid closed, Rivera wished he didn't have to breathe. The smell of the dirty scared men sickened him.

The good thing was that these people weren't asking questions. His Mexican *compadres* were always full of questions when they were smuggled. This time, the long drive would be quiet, a time for Miguel's father to clear his head. He ignored hunger. Food would be available at the end of the journey. Hours from now.

Then a strange thing. The man next to Rivera was someone he had particularly noticed and remembered. This medium-sized man with a gray beard and straight brown hair had made eye contact with him when the group arrived. His features were small, his gray eyes calm, and he looked very different from the others in his group. It was as if he were another nationality.

On the day these foreigners arrived at the smugglers camp, they had climbed down from a huge ore truck bringing them from their ocean ship. Rivera had noticed the man now pressed in the crowd next to him. His expression was different. His attitude was different. This one looked out for others, sharing with a sick man a little of the food he'd brought with him. He kept himself apart from those who had risked all the money in the world that they could earn, beg, or steal to get to America's fabled riches.

In the dark van now, Rivera felt the man's fingers touch his arm. They reached for his hand. The quiet man stood next to him in the dark. The man's hand slid into Rivera's palm. It felt dry, smooth, and warm. The man pressed Rivera's hand with steady strength. Without questioning it, Crístobal pressed back. He did not know why he accepted this odd gesture of friendship.

It was the first time since he was kidnapped that he had been touched respectfully by anyone. It made his heart pound. Tender emotions crushed inside his brain, raced to the surface. He thought of his wife. Pictured his kids. *Miguel mi 'jito . . . Miguel I am with you, son.* He held his breath to squelch the feelings again. They were too powerful. He had to.

For an hour or more, the men's hands touched from time to time to maintain the connection. The van bounced across rough ground to the border. People adjusted their position to keep standing upright. Whenever someone called "*Agua! Agua!*" (a word they had quickly learned*)*, Rivera passed the jug directly to the person in need. As they neared their destination more water was needed. Yet for the first time on a trip, they did not run out.

Reaching for Rivera's hand again, the man whispered, "Friend, I speak English."

Surprised, Rivera replied, "Good." Instinctively he took this as the sign to escape. To escape was worth anything it would cost. An English-speaking *compadre* made it seem possible.

"At the first stop, follow me. Stay close. Very dangerous. I am the man who speak to the smugglers on the American side of border. I try to break free then," Crístobal Rivera said.

"Yes. Yes!"

That was all that was said until the border was crossed and the racket of the sirens started.

"We've been discovered," Crístobal Rivera whispered, his body bathed in sweat.

"I know," the man said mysteriously.

9

Museum Music

"For almost three hundred years, this desert and mountain country of New Mexico was a Spanish and Indian world," a docent at the Palace of the Governors was telling a tour group. Miguel Rivera and Isabel Atencio stood a few feet away listening under the lofty ceiling of the Palace. It was five o'clock on Friday afternoon and they were tagging along behind a guided tour.

Isabel, dressed in a lacy Mexican blouse and a pale blue skirt that fell to the tip of her shiny dancing shoes, had tucked her black curls into a silver band circling her head. It was like a crown. Miguel was dazzled. *Why is she dressed up?*

Something special was happening at the Palace that evening, but he didn't know it and she did.

The docent continued. "Foreigners, including the citizens of the United States, were told by the Spanish governors to **Keep Out! Foreigners NOT Allowed or Welcomed!** They couldn't even trade here. Or visit as tourists like you are doing today, freely exploring the city and its treasures, and the beautiful mountains and rivers and deserts.

"Spain held tight to its empire. The king would not allow maps to circulate. He feared that strangers from other countries would follow maps and try to take over this magnificent land with its blue, beautiful skies and pink ochre earth.

"So New Mexico's only link to the outside world was the Royal Road. An eighteen-hundred-mile-long wagon trail between Mexico City and Santa Fe. Guess who was the first recorded illegal immigrant to these parts was?"

Miguel's ears pricked up.

"An American," the docent said. "A citizen from the then much smaller U.S.A. The explorer Zebulon Pike (Pike's Peak is named for him) was here spying on the Spanish government for the United States. He got caught, too!"

The docent led the tour into the next room. The tall woman wore a red velvet blouse and skirt with a Navajo silver concha belt and leather boots. Her wavy blond hair was tied back with a velvet ribbon. She looked as stately as a queen at home in the Palace.

"Now here's a list to look at. *Governors of New Mexico who Served in the Palace*," she said, reading the sign.

"Guess what?" Isabel said, huddling in a corner with Miguel and looking into his shining eyes. She tucked back under the silver band a little curl that had sprung loose. "You're NOT the first illegal immigrant into New Mexico."

Alarmed, Miguel said, "Ssh! You want me to go to prison? You have to be quiet about that, Isabel."

She giggled. The docent was explaining the duties of the territorial governors before New Mexico became a state.

"Look!" he whispered, "Names and signatures of the Mexican governors on the wall!"

"Let's see if there's a Rivera," Isabel said.

Miguel pitched his voice low so that he wouldn't bother the docent. "Armijo! Sena! Chavez! Perez . . . ! No! No Rivera. Aww!" he said, feeling sad.

In the Portrait Gallery the docent pointed out a painting of Diego Archuleta. "Señor Archuleta resisted the U.S. military occupation and control of New Mexico. Alas, he was not successful," the docent said.

"She's an Archuleta, and Diego was her ancestor," Isabel whispered. "She wishes New Mexico was still Spanish-Mexican and not Yankee-American, my mother told me."

"Really? This Palace is big. Hope I don't get lost!" he said.

"Not you! I wouldn't let that happen to you, sweet boy. Now are you ready for something special?"

"It's all special!" he said, amazed that somebody so kind and lovely was taking a kid like him around the Palace of the Governors.

"In *The Art of Ancient America* exhibit, we'll see figures of animals and people carved from stone thousands of years ago. The work comes from Mexico, Miguel, and South America."

"I've never seen anything that old."

"And they could have been made by your a-thousand-greats great-grandpa." She giggled. "Before almost anybody was sitting down to write history, they were doing these pieces."

The room they entered, unlike any of the others in the Palace, was carpeted. It was softly lit like a holy place.

"Look at all the gold!" he said when they stopped at the first exhibit, a display of jewelry.

"I think kings probably wore that jewelry. It doesn't look like things a woman would like," Isabel said, moving on to an exhibit of human figures. "Feel your nose. It's shaped like these noses. Very proud," she said.

Miguel was embarrassed.

"Look at the face inside that urn!" she said.

"Spooky!" Miguel said. "And the dog with the pointy, scary teeth!"

"It's menacing! Maybe the maker wanted to create a piece to protect something or somebody. Do you see the incense holder on top of the dog? The carved dog protected something sacred. It holds your attention, doesn't it?"

Miguel nodded. "What is that large thing with the face inside it?" he asked nervously.

"An urn. Maybe it contained the ashes of the person whose face it depicted. Maybe a memorial to someone important?"

Miguel felt shy in front of a case where he saw a male figure that he wished had worn some pants. Other figures looked ready to fight. "Those are warriors. Aren't those weird helmets they've got on?" he said.

"I think they are masks worn to scare their enemies. Sometimes they buried people with masks, a docent told us."

"Why show masks?" he said.

"Heavens, I don't know! Museums collect things for all kinds of reasons. Nobody can say for sure what the things here mean but people are studying to understand. They show what was important to the ancient people thousands of years ago."

"I think I'd have been scared a lot then." He looked at Isabel to see her reaction to his saying that.

She tilted her head and nodded, saying, "Me, too. Some of the figures don't look like real people, but maybe they were gods. Some could be objects of prayer. Like us, the ancient ones were trying to find out the meaning of life. They needed something to trust and believe in."

"Yeah . . ." And then he said sadly, "Oh, Isabel, I don't know. These things in here give me the creeps."

"But see, Miguel! They're beautifully made, aren't they? People worked hard to carve these figures out of stone."

"They were good carvers and clay workers. I never knew they made things like this so long ago."

"See how they tried to create images of people, animals, fruit?"

"Yes, I do," he said.

"They show us that all created things in the world are important."

Miguel smiled. "Do you think so?"

"I do, sweet boy."

Isabel's words helped Miguel to begin to appreciate the unusual art. Afterwards, without talking, they walked through other rooms of the Palace to see the New Mexico chapel. For the first time in months, he felt lucky and happy.

"This is what a church looked like when the Mexican governors were here. Sometimes people, afraid of being attacked, hid inside the chapels," she said. "Even so, I'd like to have lived back in the 1700s or 1800s. Families were close, passing down their ways and their thoughts to one another. Little kids learned many things from their grandparents. Our time is like watching a bunch of TV shows—one doesn't have anything to do with the other."

"Aww!" Miguel said.

"My time makes me lonely, although my family shares things we care about. But Mom hasn't taught me how to cook or to manage a business like she does. I want to live back in the olden days!"

"I want to, too!" Miguel said, gazing into her eyes. Without any moon, they looked moonlit.

"Come on, Mickey-Miguel. I want you to see the armor." She pulled his arm and led him out across the Palace garden. It was sparkling green. A whistle-thin rainfall in the morning had brightened up dry Santa Fe. She opened the door to the Segesser Hide Painting gallery. Inside she shocked him by opening a cabinet.

"It's all right! We won't hurt anything. I used to help the Palace Museum educators, Lou Ann and Libby. They had me show things to little kids who came through."

She took out a metal helmet and put it on her head. Then she gave Miguel a chain-mail breastplate and helmet.

"These are heavy!" he said, chugging around the empty gallery and slicing the air with an invisible rapier.

"How did they do it? Wear this stuff?" she said, just as the docent came in with the tour group.

"Oh, look!" the docent said in a ringing voice, making Miguel blush. She pointed him out. "We have Spanish explorers right here!"

The people on the tour laughed as Miguel and Isabel showed off the armor. He whispered to her, "Maybe I ought to wear this to Ortiz School."

"You're right. March in like a Conquistador!" Isabel said.

The docent took her group to the animal hide paintings. Isabel put away the armor and hurried to the door.

"Do we want to see these paintings?" Miguel said, hating to miss anything.

"Not right now. Let's hang out in the garden before sunset, plop on the grass. It's soft and smells good. There's a surprise for you tonight, too." They walked back into the garden.

"Is that why you wore that crown on your head?" he said shyly, sitting on the cool prickly grass under the fragrant trees. Isabel gazed into his eyes.

"Right! The Palace has invited a mariachi band to play and visitors can dance. Paul, the man who played General Don Diego de Vargas, the great explorer, will be here to introduce the musicians and me. I'm going to try to do a flamenco dance."

Looking at her he felt he was suddenly sickeningly and desperately—not just madly—in love. He had talked about her so much at home that his mother finally told him to be quiet. "Shut up, Miguel, honey. You making me crazy!"

He couldn't help thinking of asking Isabel to marry him when he turned fifteen. He'd be twelve in less than ten months. He could marry at fifteen or sixteen. Or maybe fourteen? No. He sighed. Fifteen. A long time from now!

They settled on the grass. "When you come to a museum, you learn what's precious. The things here are precious and so are you."

He shook his head. "Come on, Isabel! I'm not precious. But now I do think my country of Mexico is a pretty good country! I was ashamed of it before."

"It's beautiful, Daddy says. I want to go there one day."

"I'll take you . . ." he said under his breath, afraid she'd hear but taking a little chance anyway.

She looked at him thoughtfully. "Maybe next summer my folks will travel with you and me to Mexico City." There was silence, and then she said, "How do you feel now about living in New Mexico . . . about belonging?"

"I don't know. I'm trying to feel better." He wanted to please her.

"At my coronation in the cathedral as a Spanish princess in the Fiesta de Santa Fe Queen's Court, the archbishop told us to be ambassadors of goodwill in Santa Fe, to help all our people—the Indians, the Hispanics, and the Anglos—to feel a part of our city. Everybody is welcome here! I love that idea!"

"It sounds good . . ." Miguel said, a bit doubtfully.

"I worked on a play about it with Ortiz School's drama teacher.

Do you know Miss Jordan?"

He shook his head no.

"We'll do it for the kids at Ortiz soon. But before the play opens, I *could* talk to your class about brotherhood. Kids just get mixed up. They do whatever mean kids do when they don't even know why."

Miguel, scared of what the mean kids would say if she came to school, answered fast. "No! You don't have to do that."

She suddenly looked serious. "Miguel. It's really up to you. Not me or anyone else. Next time your teacher asks you to share something with the rest of the class, talk about the Palace Museum. Tell what it does for you," she demanded. "Try it now."

Miguel blushed, his mind blank.

"Don't be scared, dear Miguel," she said, beaming at him.

"Um, let's see. The Palace of the Governors makes me feel that I, a Mexican boy not born here, can still live in Santa Fe. I am not trash to be swept away from the Plaza or anywhere else."

"Of course not!"

"I have both the Spanish and the Indian blood, making me a real New Mexican!" he said, all at once thrilled by his own words.

"Good! Right! I am only Spanish, with years of history and tradition, of course, but you're both. Indian people have been in this land thousands of years. You're as old as the mountains, I bet," she said.

Miguel smiled at that.

"Here comes the handsome Don Diego de Vargas. You wait inside the museum, okay?" said Isabel, bending forward and kissing his cheek.

Astonished, he threw his arms around her and kissed her back. Then he ran inside, his face burning, his heart pounding.

He still wanted to see the time line in the main hall. It showed how New Mexico fit in with the history of the rest of the world. He stopped there and then turned around, looking everywhere he could see. This place was telling him **Yes!** not *No!* He was like a bird unfurling its wings for the first time. Maybe soon he could fly.

I'm going to find out something here that I can do with my whole life. Maybe be a photographer and take pictures of all the different kinds of

kids in the world to show people. Maybe I'll be a teacher like Mr.
Springley and show my pictures so kids'll understand . . .

The air was suddenly split by a trumpet blast. Miguel jerked.
The museum walls reverberated with the music of guitars, banjos,
violins, and trumpets and the rich voices of men singing. The
mariachis marched into the museum from the street. Miguel
rushed out to the garden.

"Mexican music, Mickey-Miguel! Mariachis!" Isabel said.

Men dressed in slim black suits trimmed with silver studs and
crimson embroidery on the shoulders and down the pants legs
paraded past Miguel. They were handsome and wore polished
black boots and huge felt sombreros trimmed with gold and silver.

Don Diego de Vargas announced, "Mariachi Tenampa from
Albuquerque!"

People rushed from the galleries into the garden. The musicians
cooed and chirped like birds and all nine men were singing except,
of course, for the two trumpet players.

"Come on! Can I teach you to dance?" Isabel said.

"I love this music! I heard this group at the Spanish Cultural
Center, too!" Miguel said. "Then they came to my school last year
and played for us. It is my best, my favorite music. I forgot, Isabel.
I want to be a mariachi trumpet player."

The Friday evening museum-goers began to sway with the
music and some of them were dancing on a wooden platform laid
over the grass.

"Let's dance!" she said.

"It's happy music. But, Isabel, no! I'm afraid to dance. I'm too
young. Way too young."

"Nobody's too young to dance. It's not necessary to be scared of
dancing. It's only necessary you give it a try!" she said, melting his
heart with her smiles and taking his hand into her velvety soft,
smooth one.

And although he was very glad nobody else his age was there
watching, he did give it a try. He was, after all, dancing with a New
Mexican princess.

10

Getting Free Fast

Sunrise in Arizona. Crístobal Rivera stood outside the van. It had been surrounded by patrol cars and helicopters with sirens and flashing lights and forced to stop. Rivera glanced at the sky—white and thin and as fragile as glass.

The van stood on a stretch of Highway 90. The confused and frightened workers were pulled out of the van. Twenty-seven men were commanded to sit on the hard dry ground by the Border Patrol. The angry masked captain and his ferocious muscled driver were now among them. Their guard dog, a gray pit bull, was shot and lay dead on the side of the road.

Crístobal Rivera glanced at his English-speaking friend. Twenty-five American border guards and officers, rifles in their hands, held them prisoners. Four officers were locking handcuffs on their wrists.

Rivera knew that the smuggler captain carried ammunition and guns in his van, but he had messed up and fallen asleep in the car. That was Rivera's guess. Even so fierce an adversary as the brutal captain saw the odds defeated him. He was trapped meat.

Hawks circled above. The desert wind blew a shower of dust in their faces. Rivera put his hands out in front of him, surrendering. This is it, he thought—prison in the U.S. After serving the sentence, deportation back to Mexico.

Or is freedom possible?

He stepped out of rank, sensing that the man he'd made friends with, was behind him. He raised his hands and shouted. The

Americans raised their guns.

"I was kidnapped. A slave for almost three years. I know this operation."

The smuggler captain's eyes widened. Rivera felt their murderous threat. He stepped into the center of the two opposing groups. "Please let me talk. This man, he is with me, too."

The new friend stepped beside him. He nodded in agreement.

The captain of the guards, a black man with fierce eyes and bent posture as if he carried weight on his enormous shoulders, came forward. He spoke in Spanish to the two men. "Come with me. You can be safe if you tell the truth. Otherwise it's prison and deportation," he said. "I know who you are, Crístobal Rivera. We have been looking for you."

At these words, Rivera stumbled forward and fell on his knees. The blood rushed to his head. Tears gushed from his eyes and he trembled and could not get himself back up on his feet.

The man beside him stepped past Rivera and went toward the captain. Rivera, alone, was so terrified he thought his heart would leap into his mouth. But the captain was speaking to the stranger. Then he gestured Rivera towards him. Rivera stumbled ahead and finally reached the American Border Patrol's side of the road.

He heard the captain mutter, "Your idea worked, Lieutenant Miller Williams. Good!"

Crístobal Rivera's eyes widened in shock. *LIEUTENANT? Was the man he had made friends with an INS agent?* Rivera became so dizzy he stumbled again and fell forward. He was exhausted, starving, and too terrified to believe the sudden change in his fortune. It was like a story that couldn't be true.

But it was. He was taken to a patrol car and allowed to sit down after all the hours standing and the hard labor the day before.

The officer asked for detailed information. Rivera gave it with his whole heart. An hour later he was taken to a base of operations where he was given a solid meal, a hot shower, clean towels, and a warm bed to sleep in under American guard and protection.

Lieutenant Miller Williams came to see him later. "You can try to contact your family. The INS has information locating them in Santa Fe. For the time being you'll be detained in Arizona, but the future looks promising. You may be able to obtain your legal immigrant card, the green card, for giving witness against this gang of smugglers. We've been after their tail for a long time."

"How did you know to speak to me in the van?" Rivera said to the man.

"My Mexican half-brother was kidnapped like you, by these same men. Only they murdered him. Viciously. He was thrown out like trash from a smuggler's truck. Found on the road. My only brother. All others in my family are gone. I promised his spirit I would do something to overcome the defeat of his death. I would free another man enslaved like him. I came to the smugglers' camp for this purpose. I believed it firmly. I prayed. I thought. I planned. And when I went to the smugglers' camp, I saw you immediately. Your suffering was obvious. It felt like a heavy coat that I could not take off until I succeeded in freeing you."

"My God! My own father—a man who promised to be with me all his life—once told me that *his* only brother had been lost to criminals. It was not the same way, of course, but it was, I think, the same thing."

Miller Williams did not reply, but his eyes glistened with tears.

Crístobal remembered, too, that his father had always touched his hand when speaking with him. Years after his father was gone, Crístobal relied on the fatherly love he was given.

"My father got me through these terrible long months in the camp."

His father's hands were as memorable as his face. They had never struck him. They had never failed him. They had held on to him whenever he was scared.

"This was planned with my INS unit," Williams said. "I never doubted we would succeed. The coyotes are locked up. There will be a trial and you will testify."

Crístobal Rivera nodded. "I want my son to hear my testimony and my little daughters, too."

"The American government will deal with the unfortunate workers who came to this sad end miles and miles from their homes across the Atlantic.

11

Getting Out of There Fast

Even though Miguel had told Isabel Atencio not to dare come to Ortiz School to speak to his class, he discovered her in the building one morning. It was a week after their visit to the Palace Museum. He'd come running into school and saw her in the dramatic arts room. She was wearing a slim black dress and red roses entwined in her dark shiny curls. The sight took his breath away.

Isabel raised her head to catch him looking at her. "Miguel! Come in here!" she said, beaming. "We're doing the play I helped write. Look at the set! Isn't it beautiful!"

He stuck his head around the corner of the doorway and peeked in. On the small, raised stage colorful canvas flats had been set up, a backdrop for the drama.

"This is our play on racial harassment and prejudice, and YOU know about that. Everybody in Ortiz School today gets to see it. It's going to tell how Hispanics and Mexican kids feel about each other and WHY. The eighth graders are in it. And two high school actors. I'm playing the part of a mother of two Mexican kids in Ortiz School. The drama's about the rivalry between them and two *New* Mexican kids. Remember? I wrote it with Cookie Jordan and she said she wanted to present it. Have you met her?"

"No, Isabel!" he said in a cranky voice. "I have to go upstairs to my class. I can't be late."

Ever since the thrilling, almost unbelievable telephone call from his father on Monday at 6:34 p.m. letting his astonished family know that he was alive in Arizona, Miguel was as jumpy as a raven on the ground. Waiting to see Dad, who was supposed to be coming home soon, was driving him crazy.

"You've got at least five minutes before the bell. Get in here!" shouted the petite Isabel, pulling on him.

"Stop it, girl!"

"No!"

So he had to meet the drama teacher. She was a beautiful black woman, who gave him a big smile, "Oh, good! You can help us with the lights, Miguel. One of our best helpers is sick today . . . throwing up and you know . . . everything. Guess it's going around. Poor kid! We're desperate for help," Miss Jordan said with all the authority of a teacher.

It made Miguel mad, as if he didn't have anything important to do himself. "I gotta go to my classes," he said.

"No, you don't! The principal gives an automatic excuse for anyone working on the play today. You show him what to do, Isabel. Steve Hannah, the stage manager, will be here in a minute to help you, too," Cookie Jordan said in her husky voice. She turned away and continued arranging chairs in the small auditorium. The walls were painted with murals in dark colors, and it certainly didn't look like any schoolroom he had seen before.

Miguel groaned, but he was hooked. Isabel took his backpack and jacket and put it in a locker along with hers. She showed him where the lighting board was. Billy McIntire, from the College of Santa Fe, came and showed him the lights. It was interesting to Miguel but he was still cranky. All day long the play was performed over and over again. The actors played the parts of boys on their way to school. They were harassed and teased and insulted and beaten up by other kids.

Each class in Ortiz Middle School came to see it. At the end of the half-hour performance, the students, their teachers, and some mothers and homework tutors from St. Bede's Church remained to discuss the play.

Cookie Jordan started out by saying, "Does any of this kind of stuff happen at Ortiz?"

Then the real stories of the kids would come out. Both girls and boys told about angry, harsh, mean words they had heard kids say to one another. Miguel noticed that he did not hear disagreement or criticism of the play from any of the mean students he had to put up with every day.

The play was embarrassing because it talked right out loud about the things kids did that terrified him or hurt his feelings.

Isabel, her face blooming with excitement, whispered to him in the afternoon, "See! We can get rid of some of the prejudice if we just KNOW what it is and talk honestly about it. Sam Anderson says we'll never get rid of all the prejudice kids have. I guess he's right. So many of them get off on it. But if we talk about prejudice honestly, we can deal with it and make things better."

"I don't know about that," Miguel had to say.

"Someday you could even get to be Joey Jeter Cortés's friend."

"Oh, yeah? I'm going to beat him up as soon as I can."

Isabel looked stricken. "Miguel! Are YOU going to be the only one in Ortiz School who doesn't get the message of this play?"

"Isabel . . ." he whined. "Don't say that, okay?"

A wilted rose that was dangling by its stem dropped out of her hair and landed on the dusty floor. Miguel quickly stooped to pick it up. She grabbed it from him and tossed it in a trash can as if it were nothing to her at all.

"Miguel Rivera! You listen with an open mind to this last performance for me! Okay? Promise to try." She was angry.

Why'd she have to be here today? On Friday?

The performance went on. Miguel squashed his feelings and, for her sake, tried to be a little more open to the play. After all she was a Fiesta Spanish Princess, and his own, private museum guide, and . . . a whole lot more than that.

Sitting next to him after the last performance, she whispered, "Did you get it this time?" Her small hand clutched his. "Miguel?" she pleaded.

"Yes. Yes. Yes!" he said, still grouchy on the outside but moved on the inside. The story of the new kids from Mexico and the things that happened to them in Santa Fe and how the bad things finally got better did touch him.

Isabel sighed with satisfaction. "Aww, you're just nervous because your father's finally coming home, and you have to wait. When is it now?"

"Not until next week, they said yesterday. I was hoping it was right away. They don't want us to come to Arizona. Mom wanted to; so did I!"

"It won't be long," Isabel said, hoping it was true.

"It IS long. He's in a hospital because he was suffering from pains in his stomach and they were doing tests. We talk to him every day. He has to give the border people information while he's there, too. I want him here now, Isabel! Now!"

"I know . . . I know. So do I! It's terrible to have to wait."

When the last bell rang, Miguel grabbed his pack and jacket and ran out of school. Crossing the threshold of the door he saw the yellow bus but his attention was suddenly drawn to a man standing on the grass.

He was terribly thin, his white shirt open at the neck. The man was staring at Miguel as he burst through the door with a lot of other kids.

12

A Surprise to Remember Forever

"Miguel Rivera!" the man called, vigorously waving his hands.

Miguel stopped, blocking the other students. But they were staring, too, at the man with the exhausted, sad eyes, who was smiling with incredible joy and happiness.

Miguel caught his breath.

"*Hijito!* I come to the school to find you, Miguel."

"Dad? Dad! *Papa!*" Miguel shouted, dropping his pack and jacket and running. "You're here? Papa!" He laughed and cried and ran into the arms of Crístobal Rivera.

"You grew! You're so big!" said his father, who didn't look as tall as Miguel remembered. He tightened his arms around Miguel, tears in his eyes.

The Ortiz students stared. "You know anything about this new kid, Miguel Rivera? Or his father who's come to school?" they asked one another.

Suddenly Joey Jeter Cortés was shouting everything he knew. "Miguel's father was the prisoner of a gang of smugglers. They're called coyotes. They sneaked workers over the border for years and years! The Border Patrol was trying to catch them. And last Sunday the INS cracked their ring. Caught them on this side of Arizona! They freed Miguel's dad! Look! They brought him to Santa Fe today, to Miguel and his family. My dad told me! He's a lieutenant in the INS."

The kids surrounded Joey Jeter, who was another new kid, ask-

ing him all kinds of questions.

"How are you, my boy?" Crístobal said to Miguel.

"I'm fine, Papa! How are you? How'd you get here? We didn't know you were coming today. We went crazy waiting to see you!"

"So did I! I begged them to let me out of the hospital. They were pretty nice. They wanted me to come home, too. So this morning they put me on a plane from Tucson with two border guards and flew us to Albuquerque. You know I never got there two years ago? I was kidnapped. Captured on a street near the El Paso Bus Station. I never came to Albuquerque at all."

"Oh, Dad! We were so sad, so scared!" Miguel said, noticing the warm brown of his father's eyes. His wonderful smile made Miguel's heart fill with the most happiness he'd ever felt. "We never knew what happened, Dad. It was terrible! Everybody cried and cried!"

"I know. I know. It killed me every time I think of it, and I think of it those two years all the time. Anyway the INS gave the border guards a car to drive me from Albuquerque over here to Santa Fe. Boy, it's beautiful here! Look at those mountains! All gold!"

"It's aspens. They turn gold. Everybody loves them, they're so beautiful," Miguel said.

"See the van. Right there!" Crístobal pointed to a green van marked INS behind the line of school buses. All the kids were stopped, everybody watching with surprise and interest at Miguel and his beaming father.

Miguel saw the INS officers standing near the curb, too. His mind was a whirlwind. He couldn't think. Finally he realized the kids were standing around just watching him and his dad. A boy he didn't know picked up Miguel's pack and jacket and brought them to him. Miguel suddenly had to tell everybody and shout the news.

"Hey! Meet my father! This is Crístobal Rivera. My dad! See! He's come home after he was gone for way over two years. I didn't know where he was. We were so scared!"

The Ortiz School kids applauded and shouted, "Hooray!

Hooray! Welcome to Santa Fe, Mr. Rivera! Welcome home, Mr. Rivera! Welcome home!"

And then Joey Jeter Cortés ran up to Miguel, his face redder than the crimson it already was, and said, "I'm glad your father's come back." He looked down, unable to say the true thought in his mind. The play had brought that thought home to him. He wished he could say *I'm sorry!* But he couldn't do that. So he said, "I'm glad your dad's come home to you, Miguel," two more times. Somehow he was hoping Miguel Rivera might guess the other things that he meant.

Miguel stared. How could he say anything to this rat? But he happened to look away for a second to catch his thoughts and saw Isabel standing in the doorway. She might have been crying, her face was so red.

But she smiled at him, nodding her head up and down. So Miguel Rivera took his cue from her. "Thanks a lot," he said to Joey Jeter Cortés with feeling.

Joey Jeter then announced to the kids standing around that it was the hardest case that his father, the lieutenant, had ever worked on. He told me that," Joey Jeter said.

Arms around each other's shoulder, Miguel and Crístobal started down the walk crowded with teachers, tutors, custodians, and students.

"We'll go camping together, right Pop?" Miguel said, remembering Albert suddenly, who called his father Pop. "I got a friend in Albuquerque named Albert. You'll meet him," he said.

"We will go camping, you and me, Miguel."

They climbed into the van. Two officers took the front seats. The Ortiz kids rushed forward and cheered as the van drove off toward the center of Santa Fe.

"Does Mom know you're here?"

"Not yet!" Crístobal said. "Think she'll be surprised?"

"Oh, boy! Oh, boy! And the twins! And María Contenta . . . she never stops asking for you, Papa. Never! But she's doing good. She's on anti-seizure medicine. She goes to school like the rest of us now. They'll be in Señor Fantastico's store when we get there. Hey! Think the driver would take us through the Plaza on our way? So you can see it. I have to show you a special place there. The ancient Palace of the Governors. It was a fortified palace, and now it belongs to the people of Santa Fe and it's just a little out of the way."

"As long as it doesn't take us any longer," Crístobal said. "I got to see my Rosa." His voice cracked. "I was afraid somebody would steal her away from me . . ."

"She was way too busy, Dad!"

"We can drive to the Plaza if you'd like," the driver said. "We're assigned to help you get around."

Miguel thought a minute, then shook his head. "No, no, sir. Thanks. It'll take too much time and I want Dad to see everything in the museum. It's important. We can do it tomorrow, Dad," he said, smiling at the wonderful word *tomorrow* in connection with the wonderful word *Dad*. Then he noticed the shopping bags that were in the car with them. "What's all this?" he said, marveling that he could just turn his head and see his father's face. It was so easy, but it felt like a miracle to be here with Dad on an ordinary day like today.

"The man who rescued me bought presents. For me to give. Presents for everybody. Beautiful ones! He got the tent for camping, too," Crístobal said, pointing to a green box. There were sudden tears in his eyes that Miguel saw. They filled him with deep feelings of tenderness and relief. He knew that he and his dad were the most important thing of all, *simpático*.

"As soon as I get my driver's license—with my new green legal immigrant card the INS gave me—then you and I will go to the mountains and sleep in the quiet of the trees. Just like I promise on that night long ago, *mi 'jito*. I think we will hear the music of the stars. You have to listen carefully to hear their singing."

The words reverberated like music. They were new and thrilling like discoveries in the Palace of the Governors had been. The world that had been miserably and cruelly tilted out of whack for so long righted itself. Like a freed bird, Miguel sailed into the long dreamed-of happiness of *la familia Rivera* in Santa Fe.

The INS car turned on Guadalupe Street, heading for the the México Fantastico Bargain Bazaar, a big adobe building with a white portal where shoppers gathered.

"Hey, Pop! Over to the left, look!" Miguel yelled. "Turn in! Turn in! Good. Thanks. Oh! Look! Look! See? There's Mom and the girls!"

His dark eyes widened at the sight of a big white van in the parking lot. "The Channel 4 TV truck is here. And Carla Aragón. Who told her about this? Oh boy, I gotta get out and help Mom speak her English."

The van skidded to a stop on gravel. Crístobal and Miguel leaped out. Rosa and her girls were jumping up and down and waving at them.

The reunion of Crístobal Rivera with his family was shown on Channel 4 Eyewitness News that evening. Miguel himself got to tell the story of his father's return to Carla Aragón, his mother's favorite reporter. Rosa was too busy hugging and kissing Crístobal to talk. Kids from Ortiz School saw it on the news. Isabel called him to say, "Mickey-Miguel, you're famous now."

Albert King in Albuquerque called, too.

He said, "I saw you, Miguel! I never saw anybody I know on TV before! I feel famous, too!"

"Joey Jeter called to say he saw me," Miguel said.

"That stinker? Wow. And guess what?" Albert said.

"What?"

"You didn't look too funny, Miguel," he said.

Miguel laughed. "Albert?" he said. "You ain't seen nothing yet!"